Hunters in the Fog

Hunters in the Fog
War Diary to Screenplay

Jim Stallings

with

Consultant James B. Stallings, Sr.
(Lt. Col. USAF, Retired)

iUniverse, Inc.
New York   Lincoln   Shanghai

Hunters in the Fog
War Diary to Screenplay

All Rights Reserved © 2003 by Jim Stallings

No part of this book may be reproduced or transmitted in any form or by any means, graphic, electronic, or mechanical, including photocopying, recording, taping, or by any information storage retrieval system, without the written permission of the publisher.

iUniverse, Inc.

For information address:
iUniverse
2021 Pine Lake Road, Suite 100
Lincoln, NE 68512
www.iuniverse.com

ISBN: 0-595-29841-9 (Pbk)
ISBN: 0-595-66064-9 (Cloth)

Printed in the United States of America

For My Father & Mother

Children of the Great Depression
Young Adults of World War II
Parents & Grandparents during the Cold War
A Generation of Quiet & Loving Heroes

"We're all going to live till we die."

—James B. Stallings, Sr.
(Lt. Col. USAF, Retired)

Content

Note to Reader xi

The War Diary: "My Stretch in the Air Corps
                of the U.S.A. Army in the E.T.O." 1

The Screenplay: Hunters in the Fog 55

Note to Reader

My father kept a mission diary during his 300 combat hours and 81 missions as a P-47 pilot in England during WWII. His tour in the E.T.O. (European Theater of War) centered around D-Day and its aftermath, from April to September 1944. During this period he also corresponded with his new wife, Millie Baker Stallings, my mother; they exchanged letters on nearly a daily basis. I'm not sure my father or mother has ever written so much in so short a time since that combat tour in 1944. Apparently those letters were destroyed for privacy reasons after the war. The mission diary survived.

When Dad returned from the war, the Army Air Corps Intelligence kept his diary and combat films for review; these were eventually returned to him as was the custom. Along with his flight jacket and leather helmet, the combat films and diary and other paraphernalia gathered dust in a closet under the stairs in our house. I and my two sisters Lynn and Denise were born after the war, and these war memorabilia became part of a gradual evolution of an almost legendary and misty history we could barely understand. My father would answer questions about his war tour, but he was not by nature and inclination one to dwell on the past. My father returned to civilian life, but the Korean War brought him back into service in the U.S. Air Force. He decided to make a career in the Air Force. He served in the Strategic Air Command in the early 60s and in Viet Nam in the late 60s. He retired in 1970. Over the years, as we moved around the U.S.A. in the Air Force the old combat films were tossed out along with the mildewed, rotting leather fighter jacket and helmet. But the medals and a few scrapbooks survived along with the War Diary.

In the early 1990s I had begun to write screenplays and novels. I wanted to develop my skills at adapting historical or fictional narratives into film screenplays. I set out developing "Hunters in the Fog" primarily from Dad's diary and conversations with him. We also found a collection of diary excerpts from other pilots of that era quite useful in highlighting dramatic moments in a dive bomber's tour (see: *Eagles of Duxford: The 78th Fighter Group in World War II* by Garry L. Fry). I hoped to have the screenplay ready for marketing prior to the 50th anniversary of D-Day in

1994. That was accomplished but as a tyro in the trade I didn't realize the amount of advance time required for promoting a time-sensitive film. When I began to circulate the screenplay, the film industry was already well beyond any active interest given the production times required. So, reluctantly I shelved the project except for more general circulation as a screen play about fighter pilots in war.

This book is meant to celebrate and honor my father and mother's participation in that difficult time in WWII. While the timeliness for film production may be past in terms of a 50th anniversary, what they accomplished is simply timeless and echoes universal, archetypal narrative themes. The warrior separated from his wife in war, urgently using every skill and power at his disposal to survive that war and do his honorable best, and return at last to his home and loving wife. This goes back to earliest human experience, and of course in the case of Western literature to the classic tale of Ulysses, his warrior years in the Trojan war, and his difficult "odyssey" of return to home and family.

"Hunters in the Fog" looks into the mysterious questions of luck and fate in war. Why is it certain men, regardless of their refined skills in war, fall victim to death, chopped short in youth? My father turns over that question in his diary. He notes the near misses to himself and other pilots, the mysterious accidents, the horror of fiery death and the strange beauty and suspense of aerial warfare. With his advice I crafted a play that looks into these fateful questions through the lives of four pilots who fly in the same flight formation supporting one another. Inspired in part by the classic dramatis personae of the Dumas' *The Three Musketeers* I found a similar range of personalities central to exploring these age old questions of fate and luck in a P-47 dive bomber flight of four different men.

In this first edition of the book there may be a number of technical and copy editing errors; these are all my doing as this work was assembled under wraps as a gift to my father and mother. I did not have the benefit of their excellent memories for review. Let me apologize now for any mistakes historical, technical or otherwise. Here I want to thank my sister Lynn for her confidential recovery and return of illustrative photos from the family archives. Thanks also to Laurie Stallings for her patient and able photography (see her absract expressionist art work at www.lauriesart.net). And thank you to my good buddy in the writing business, Charles Melville Thiesen, who ably assisted with computer formatting issues.

My father's penmanship like so many of his generation was and is excellent. With the exception of a couple of lines blurred in photocopying, ninety-nine percent was readable. However, again, all errors in transcription from my father's handwritten diary are my own. Needless to say, without his expert consultation, the screenplay would not have been possible to develop in most of it technical and many of its dramatic situations. The best of this work is to his credit.

Jim Stallings

Diary
*My Stretch in the Air Corps
of the U.S.A. Army in the E.T.O.*

2nd Lt. James B. Stallings marries Millie Baker on December 14, 1943, in Sarasota, Florida; two months later he ships out for England and a tour of duty as a combat P-47 pilot.

1st Lt. James B. Stallings in the cockpit of his P-47. He flew 300 hours of combat in 81 missions during the months before and after D-Day. His exploits earned him nine medals including the DFC (Distinguished Flying Cross).

The Standard Diary for any Year or
My Stretch in the Air Corps of the U.S.A. Army in the E.T.O.*

[signed:] **James B. Stallings**

* European Theater of Operation

[opposing page a poem hand copied]
composed by Margaret Scruton

For Honor and For Her

Somewhere, a woman, thrusting fear away,
Faces the future bravely for your sake;
Toils on from dawn to dark; from day to day;
Fights back her tears, nor heeds the bitter ache;
She loves you, trusts you, breathes in prayer your name;
Soil not her faith in you, by sin or shame.

Somewhere a woman—mother—sweetheart—wife—
Waits betwixt hopes and fears for your return;
Her kiss, her words, will cheer you in the strife;
When death itself confronts you, grim and stern;
But let her image all your reverence claim,
When base temptations scorch you with their flame.

Somewhere a woman watches—filled with pride;
Shrined in her heart, you share a place with none.
She toils, she waits, she prays, till side by side,
You stand together when the battle's done.
Oh keep for her dear sake a stainless name,
Bring back to her a manhood free from shame.

[handwritten comment by James B Stallings]

In memory of my wife and mother.

      *   *   *

Joined cadets July 10, 1942
Called to active duty Feb. 3, 1943
Nashville Classification Center Feb, 1943
Preflight, Maxwell Field, Ala. Mar & April, 1943
Primary, Union City, Tenn May & June, 1943
Basic, Malden, Missouri July & Aug, 1943
Advanced, Marianna, Fla. Sept & Oct., 1943
Graduated—Wings & Gold Bars Nov 3, '43
O.T.U.—Venice, Fla Dec & Jan, 1944
Ft. Hamilton, N.Y.—P.of E.—Feb 12 to Mar 21,'44
Ile de France—ship we sailed to England on Mar 13-21, 1944
Stone, Eng.—Air Corps Replacement Center
Atcham, Eng.—Training field (to brush up before going on operational duty)
Duxford, Eng.—Our home (ops station-this is 8 miles below Cambridge)

March 12, 1944

Tonight we shouldered our packs and marched down to the private dock at Ft. Hamilton and boarded a harbor boat that took us to Pier#59, where the Queen Mary and the Ile de France were docked. We were given coffee and donuts by the Red Cross (good folks) and then were given our quarters on the Ile de France. We were lucky and were on "A" deck which was very good. We also had rooms that were formerly used by ocean going honeymooners only we had 22 in our room. We couldn't get to sleep and all of us seemed to stay awake all nite.—

Morning of the 13th

We all got up and had breakfast at 7:30 as this was our sitting. They had to rotate, as it took five sittings for each meal before everyone had their food. We saw the Statue of Liberty move past abut 8:30 and we knew we were on our way.

The next few days are a series of eating, sleeping, and standing on deck watching the wind and waves. The first three days were very rough and about 1/3 of the paddlefeet (ground officers) and nurses got seasick. Only about five of our 200 pilots got seasick and then only for a short time. On March 17, we passed the Gripsholm, the exchange ship going toward the U.S.

We had life boat drills every morning and soon got right into the routine. We had no trouble with subs as the ship could out run them. We also had everything in the way of gun protection, including...a variety of cannons...and rocket guns for anti-aircraft.

March 18, 1944.

We were circled by a Liberator on anti-sub patrol and knew we didn't have long to wait before sighting land.

March 1, 1944

Oh Happy Day!! This morning when I looked out I saw the beautiful coast of Ireland off our port side and never was there a prettier picture. Its resemblance to a picture was remarkable. Big bare bluffs and on the coast a few light houses, all covered by a low overcast that seemed to hang like a veil over this lovely place. If only I could have been a painter to try to do justice to that scene, as if there was ever a painter that could do justice to that part of God's world this morning.

About noon we dropped anchor in a big harbor that was busy looking after ships and war materials. There were aircraft carriers, battle ships, freighters and big troop transports all over the harbor. We are to stay on deck till tomorrow.

March 22, 1944

This morning about 8:30 we loaded on a lighter from the ship and were carried to the train station. We immediately loaded into the coaches, where we were given donuts, coffee, cigarettes, chewing gum and candy by the Red Cross. Remind me to contribute more to those people. We didn't have long to wait before our train pulled out from the little harbor town where we had dropped anchor. This port was Greenook and continued through Glasgow, heading in a southeastern direction. We hoped, of course that we were going to be based near London but no one knew where we were headed.

I always miss Millie but much more when I see beautiful things and wish she could see them too. I have really wished for her today to see all these beautiful things. Our coaches were almost like American coaches but their box cars (called goods wagons) are about 15 feet long and are about 1/4 as long as our box cars and only hold about 1/5 as much as at home.

There are big beautiful hills and mountains covered with wild flowers and grass. The small stone houses with thatched roofs and country like you read about in books, all this rolls by our window and no wife or family to share it. This is one reason why war is such hell—you never get time to appreciate the things God put here to have appreciated.

March 23, 1944

Stone, England

Today we are at a little place called Stone near Stafford on Trent. This is an air crew replacement center for fighter and bomber personnel. We arrived here last night after a train ride from Glasgow, Scotland. We got off into an English blackout and it was plenty black. We were carried in G.I. trucks to our camp here and given our quarters and a good hot meal which was wonderful after eating C rations all day.

We will be here long enough to get a few lectures, any necessary shots (one for me) and get our assignment. We have very little to do except go eat and attend a couple of lectures a day. I got my $110 dollars changed into English money which was about £27-10 or about 27 pounds, 10 shillings.

March 27, 1944

Atcham, near Shrewsbury

Today we left Stone and arrived at Atcham, a pilots training field, where we are to brush up on our flying before we go on operational duty. This field is about 6 miles south of Shrewsbury, a town abut the size of Montgomery, Alabama.

We have very good food here but our barracks are pretty cold. We also have to go about 300 yards to take a shower. However we have a nice officers club and two big snooker tables, a picture show every other night and a snack and liquor bar. I have found why nobody likes this English beer—the stuff is awful—it couldn't have come out of a horse as it would have killed him. We have about a 100 hours here of ground school which doesn't make me happy.

April 8, 1944

London, England

We arrived from Atcham this afternoon and got our first look at London. We came in at the Liverpool Street Station and took the underground (English for subway) to Piccadilly Circus (Square) and got a room at the Jules Club, a club for officers, operated by the American Red Cross.

We looked over the area around our club and saw some of the old historical places. We visited London Tower and Waterloo Bridges, the Tower of London, the Thames River and looked at damage caused by the blitz. Saw the Houses of Parliament, Buckingham Palace and the British Museum building closed for the duration. We saw many other places too numerous to mention.

April 10, 1944

Duxford, England

Arrived at our operational station which is a field at Duxford, about 10 miles south of Cambridge—famous for its school for boys—"Cambridge Univ." This is an old R.A.F. field and our quarters are excellent. We live in big brick houses, three men to each room. Lt. Dicks and Hosford are my room-mates and are good boys.

We have food better than any civilian can get over here and plenty of it. It is served by men who bring the meal in three courses, soup, main meal, dessert.

We flew this afternoon, after arriving here just before noon, even before our equipment arrived. We practiced battle formation and show formation. I won't be long now, I'm a thinking!!

        # flak encountered
        * E/A encountered
        † failed to return—probably {K.I.A., M.I.A. or N.Y.R.}

From this point on I am only going to enter my experiences on operational missions until I have finished my tour of 200 (cross out: 300) hours.

Increased to 300 hours on 1st of May.

    P.O.W.—Prisoner of War
    N.Y.R.—Not yet reported (usually M.I.A.)
    Libs—Liberators or B-24's
        > Big Friends
    Forts—Flying Fortresses or B-17

E/A—Enemy Aircraft
A/D—Airdrome or airfield
Big Friends—bombers
Little Friends—friendly fighters
Box of bombers—60 planes
R/V—rendezvous or make contact
Landfall—where (point) we pass from sea over land
109 or ME 109—German Messerschmidt 109 Fighter
190 or FW 190—German Focke Wolfe 190 Fighter
Bogie—unidentified aircraft

April 12, 1944 * # †

"My First Mission" (or where is my nerve medicine)!

My first mission was a bomber penetration mission, consisting of three Task Forces of heavy bombers. The First and Second task force was 6 boxes (60 bombers per box) of Forts (B-17) and the Third Task Force was three boxes of Libs (B-24)—540 Bombers in all. The targets were Frankfurt and Schweinfurt, both factories for enemy planes.

    We made landfall above Dunkerque proceeding over Lille where we had a lot of heavy accurate flak come up in our formation. Two planes were slightly damaged by flak here and had to return home. We made R/V (rendezvous) with Bombers about 50 miles southeast of Lille and were with them about 30 minutes. About the time we were to turn back we sighted three bogies far below us. I released my belly tank and down we went.

    The bogies turned out to be Ju.87's (Stukas). My flight leader Lt. Watkins and Capt. Hockery each selected one and went after them. Capt. Hockery's E/A (enemy aircraft) crashed into some woods and burned after he had hit it hard. Our E/A tried to make it back to his field near Saarbrucken and just as we reached it, Watkins gave it a burst into the cockpit. It crashed and burned on the edge of the airdrome (A/D).

Lt. Lamb also chased the last plane and also shot it down. We started to strafe the field but heavy ground fire changed our mind. Two planes were damaged by ground machine gun fire before our mind was changed, however. We then climbed back up and proceeded home without further trouble.

This was pretty exciting for my first mission, and I was sorry I didn't get a chance to shoot—such is the luck of a wingman. Lt. Reese in 83rd was M.I.A. (Missing In Action) from this mission.

* * *

April 13, 1944 * #

Mission #2. Bomber Penetration.

Another long mission using 150 gal. belly tank. Three Task forces of bombers—8 boxes of Forts and 4 boxes of Libs—720 bombers were dispatched to bomb Nurnberg and Wurzburg. We made R/V with bombers on time and stayed with them, giving close support for 35 minutes. Our flight bounced about 10#—109s about 20,000 ft. below us but lost them in heavy clouds.

Lt. D.R. Roberts, one of our boys, a good friend of mine, also on his second mission was shot down by F.W.-190 when he dropped about 1000 yards behind his flight. Hope he got out, but rather doubt it. Damn those Huns, anyway—

Lt. Roberts—M.I.A.
Reported P.O.W. on 7/4/44

* * *

April 16, 1944 †

Mission #3. Fighter Sweep.

This mission was what we call a "No Ball". We were to furnish area support in an area 50 miles inland to the coast and were vectored by air English Radar station to all possible bandits (enemy aircraft). This fighter sweep was carried out without sighting an E/A, though we investigated several formations that turned out to be big and little friends. B-26s and A-20s attacked several harbors and airdromes.

Lt. O'Connoll killed on local flying—in sight of the field.

* * *

April 20, 1944 #

Mission #4. Bomber Penetration.

This is a new kind of bomber mission as we are escorting P-38s who have a new transparent nose with a bombardier in them. They are highly secret and this is the first time they have been used operational. There were about 72 P-38s who were on this mission. The target was Brussels but due to a 10/10 overcast they weren't able to bomb so that the results could be photographed, and they returned without bombing. No E/A were seen but heavy, accurate flak was thrown at us at Östende as we passed out on the way home. THe flak is really pretty at twilight—if it is at someplace besides where you are.

*   *   *

April 22, 1944 #

Mission #5. Bomber Withdrawal.

We were furnishing close support for bombers who had bombed the marshalling yards (Railway yards) at Hamm. There were 8 boxes of Forts and 6 boxes of Libs—a total of 840 bombers. Made R/V with last box of Libs east of Brussels and escorted them to the Channel. One bunch of about 12 bombers turned south about Lille and dropped incendiaries on an A/D starting several fires in administrator buildings and dispersal section. They then rejoined their formation. Two Libs went down before we reached the coast and a Fort ditched in the drink shortly after passing out. We ran through heavy flak at Östende and observed moderate flak around Dunkerque.

Not Counted as a Mission
Mission # Spotter (Air-Sea Rescue)

In conjunction with the air-sea rescue service I served as a spotter over the Channel, watching for any planes going down in the water so that we may get a boat to them as quickly as possible. I was given several vectors (courses) to fly to look for possible planes in the water but saw nothing. Was finally relieved by another group after about two and half hours of circling around.

*   *   *

April 25, 1944 #

Mission #6. Bomber Penetration.

The target for today was Metz, Nancy, and two airdromes in southern France, carried out by six boxes of B-17s and 3 boxes of B-24s. We made landfall and R/V at the same time below Dieppe, turning inland by Amiens, Paris and south. We were with bombers about 30 minutes and very little flak was experienced. Our squadron sighted no E/A, but the 83rd bounced about 30+ ME-109s and got three.

We came out above Abbeville and proceeded home. I was unable to release belly tank which slowed me up. I land with 15 minutes gas supply—Rough sweating out that gas gauge something awful.

* * *

April 27, 1944 #

Mission #7. Fighter Sweep.

On this sweep we gave area support in the Paris area. We made landfall below Abbeville, proceeding south past Amiens at 18,000 feet. We saw plenty of flak around in this section. We almost flew over Paris before we saw it below us through a hole in the clouds. We went down to about 10,000 ft and I got a glimpse of the Eiffel Tower and the main section of Paris before turning east.

No E/A were sighted and we came home unmolested. Looks like the Luftwaffe is staying out of our way these days.

* * *

April 27, 1944 #

Mission #8. Bomber Penetration.

The bombers' targets for today was A/D's in southeastern France and they were bombed by 420 Forts and Libs. Made landfall and rendezvous (R/V) at Le Havre and proceeded inland. One box of Forts flew through box barrage of flak, two Forts were hit and exploded violently. No chutes were seen, so those 20 men were instantly killed. Red and white flights turned into 10 bogies following 2-Thunderbolts and they turned away and headed toward Germany like a bat outa h—

Couldn't release belly tank again so was short of gas again.

Received my first decoration today, the "Air Medal" for completing 10 sorties over enemy territory. Also received my own plane, one used by Major Munson before he finished his tour. The name of the plane is "Lady Yvonne." I'll rename it the "Millie B" sometimes soon.

* * *

April 28, 1944 # !

Mission #9. Bomber Withdrawal.

Today we had another long mission using the big belly tank. We flew out due east and made landfall at the southern part of the Frisian Islands. We continued east through "Happy Valley" (the Ruhr Valley) which is the German's heaviest flak section, and they didn't disappoint us in the least. They threw up everything except the kitchen sink.

We made R/V with the bombers which consisted of 660 planes in eleven boxes, 4 boxes of Libs and 7 boxes of Forts. We took the rear of the formation and looked after all the stragglers—most of them having one or two engines feathered. We came by pretty close to some of the bombers and the boys waved at us. They were darn glad to see us, as they probably made it back without being shot down. We stayed 15 minutes later than scheduled and had to start back because we were getting low on gas. We started home and also started letting down at the same time. We had a stiff wind from the north and it blew us further south than our course. We passed over Dunkerque at 4,000 feet (20,000 feet too low to suit me) and they gave us a good reception. The first three bursts hit just under my tail, one of the pieces knocked a hole about the size of my fist in my left wing and one about the same size just behind the motor. It went through three thicknesses of metal before it stopped. This makes more work for my poor crew chief.

My plane still gets more gas than lots of them. I landed with almost an hour's supply today and some of the fellows had to land at the coast and refuel before coming on home. Getting that belly tank off makes a big difference.

* * *

April 29, 1944

Mission #10. Bomber Penetration.

Made R/V with 2nd Task Force consisting of 240-Forts north of Le Havre, giving close support all the way in south of Paris. We were relieved there by the 56th Group and a group of P-38's who escorted the bombers over the three airdromes which were their target today. Was finally able to drop my belly tank without any trouble. Came home at about 18,000 ft., coming out below Amiens without hitting any flak areas. Also had to avoid balloon barrages over London on way home. Good gasoline consumption this trip—averaging about 85 gal. per hr.

* * *

April 30, 1944 #

Mission #11. Bomber Penetration.

We made landfall today south of Le Havre and made R/V with big friends about 50 miles NW of Paris, between Le Havre and the Cherbourg Peninsula. Our squadron gave support to the second box of Forts and the 83rd took the first box. The 83rd's big friends were bounced by about 30+ Huns and the Huns were bounced in turn by the 83rd squadron who followed them to the deck getting four destroyed, 2 probable, and 2 damaged. Our squadron was about 1/2 minute late and when we arrived all was over. Seldom does one of these fights last more than 30 seconds.

We left the bombers south of Paris and headed home. On the way we went down on an A/D but saw no planes so we didn't strafe. Lt. Hagarty and flight shot up some dummies on another A/D. Little flak on A/D, and outskirts of Paris, continuing home without further happenings.

* * *

May 1, 1944. #

Mission #12. Bomber Penetration.

Made landfall below Ostende at a little place called Nieuport proceeding inland at 20,000 ft. We passed some B-26's coming home from beating h—out of something up around Antwerp. They left their target burning, visible about 50 miles away. We R/V about 50 miles north of Rheims and escorted our big friends over the marshalling yards at Rheims. They did a good job of egg laying (for a change), encountering moderate inaccurate flak over the target. Bombers then turned for home and we escorted them to coast. No E/A was sighted, though we made one detour after some bogie which dived into the haze and we lost them.

* * *

May 7, 1944. #

Mission #13. Bomber Penetration.

We used the big 150 gal belly tank on this trip as it was a long mission. We were to R/V with 2nd Task force composed of 300 Forts but they were a little late so we took the very front of formation. They were on their way to Berlin and were far more bombers than I have ever seen. There were 1020 of our big friends on this trip and one of the largest day-light raids of the war. We escorted them beyond Hanover and were relieved by P-38s and Mustangs (P-51s) there. I turned back a little early and brought one of the new boys home who couldn't release his belly tank and was short on gas (due to drag caused by belly tank). As I missed briefing this morning, I had to come home by dead reckoning and I missed the field by about 5 miles on the 400 miles round trip, which is darn good—for me.

*   *   *

May 8, 1944. # †

Mission #14. Bomber Withdrawal.

And still another 150 gal belly tank trip—Boy is my rear—getting tired of pounding that parachute. We furnished fighter support for 420 Libs who pounded Brunswick earlier in the morning. We made landfall over an overcast and went inland south of the Walcheren Islands, continuing across the Zuider Zee and made R/V with the first box of Libs just west of Hanover. We dropped off Black and Green flights and continued to rear box to protect rear and look after stragglers. We were pulling contrails all over the sky and it was beautiful. As usual, darn it, our squadron saw no E/A, but the lucky (?) 83rd were bounced by 10+ bandits (ME-109s in this case) and lost one of their pilots who was away from the formation. The Huns also got two bombers on this pass. Darn good work for them the Huns, I'm sure. They are smart and don't attack unless they have the advantage. Some heavy inaccurate flak on eastern edge of Zuider Zee and light inaccurate at other places. The German WAAC's must have been doing the shooting today. We escorted the bombers all the way to the English coast and made sure that the stragglers didn't plunk down in the drink. One Lib had to ditch, but an Air-Sea rescue launch was almost to the spot before he landed in the water. Wonder if they even got their feet wet.

Lt. Ford—M.I.A.—83rd Sqdn.

*   *   *

May 8, 1944 #

Mission #15.

Another double mission day. We had a split mission this evening, two of our squadrons acting as bomber support and the other squadron was on Type 16 Fighter Sweep in the same area. We furnished fighter support for two boxes (120) Libs who bombed Brussels. We met them just as we made landfall at Flushing on the southern end of the Walcheren Islands. We saw some flak here and more over Brussels. The bombers took their time and dropped bombs from edge of town all across town. If they didn't hurt much I'll bet they scared hell out of a lot of folks. THey left the docks burning and then turned west, passing out at Nieuport without collecting any more flak.

*   *   *

May 9, 1944 # *

Mission #16—Bomber Escort (IN)

The 2nd and 3rd Task Forces today had Neurnberg, St. Trond, and St. Dizier for their targets. We made R/V before we made landfall at a point below Le Treport. Continued south till we were relieved by Lightnings and Mustangs after being with bombers about 45 minutes. We saw very little flak, and none at the coast when all came out. Everybody was P.O.'ed because they had to pull so much manifold pressure to stay with the colonel. A very uneventful trip altogether. Unusual number of aircraft operating along invasion coast from Cherbourg Peninsula to Frisian Islands. Many A-20s and B-26s were seen going in to keep up their good work—pounding hell out of the Germans.

      *   *   *

May 11, 1944 # * † †

Mission #17. Bomber Penetration.

This is our first mission with two 108 gal. wing tanks—carrying 521 gallons of gasoline. We flubbed our dub going out and didn't get but 8,000 ft when we made landfall below Le Havre and continued southeast, below Paris almost to the border of Switzerland.

 A group of about 10+ F.W. 190's bounced the flight just behind us and I saw some of them in a dog fight and they dove to the deck. I then saw where one of them was shot down. Two German planes were shot down and none of ours were lost. Capt. Wilkerson and Lt. Watkins took their planes down—two flights of four planes each. They destroyed three planes and damaged three more on the ground, but flak shot up four of the planes. Lt. Steele, one of our boys from Marianna had his engine shot up and went on into Switzerland and bailed out. Lt. Kosinski also had his motor shot up and had to bail out a few miles from the A/D. We last saw him on the ground waving to us, and hope he gets away and gets back to England. My right wing tank glass coupling broke and I had to come home early. I started home with only 160 gallons of gas and just made it with about 10 minutes supply of gas left. We saw a little flak, but it was moderate and inaccurate.

Lt. Steele	|
	| M.I.A.
Lt. Kosinski	|

      *   *   *

May 11, 1944

Mission #18. Bomber Withdrawal.

A short mission, a mixture of "no-ball" and fighter sweep. We went in and out at Nieuport, and met the five boxes of bombers about a hundred miles inland. We turned around there and came back with the Forts to the coast. We saw no flak which was very unusual. However we went in and out at the very best place along the invasion coast to avoid flak. This was the second mission today.

*   *   *

May 12, 1944 #! *! † one month completed—60:05 hours combat time—139:55 to go!

Mission #19. Bomber Penetration.

What a mission! We left about 10 AM and made R/V with the bomber over the channel at 20,000 ft and proceeded east, making landfall at Nieuport and continued southeast toward southern Germany. Their targets were some A/D and railway yards in southern Germany. We continued inland going forward and giving close support to the first box of bombers. We continued on out ahead sweeping the area for E/A. We had just released our belly tanks when about 40+ enemy fighters, all F.W.-190's dove through the 1st box of bombers. They continued on through with about five flights of P-47s on their tails. The E/A had more speed, due to their diving from higher altitude and we couldn't catch up with them. We got four of them who were behind the others and chased the others half way through Germany before we had to turn back because we were short of fuel. We turned back over Metz at 4,000 ft. and for about 2 minutes it seemed as if they (the flak) wouldn't let me out of town. I have been told that when you hear flak it is too close. Today I heard at least 50 bursts and felt very certain I would never get away alive—but the Lord looked after me and I got away without even a hole in my plane. I was very short on gas and had 300 miles to go. I leaned out the mixture and cut my RPM's to 1900 to conserve gas. Made it home with about 20 minutes supply, logging 4 hours for this mission. We lost one of our best flight leaders, Lt. Hagarty who had served a tour as a bomber pilot and was almost through with his tour here. He had flown about 2,000 hours when shot down. This is our third man in two days—which isn't good! We got four planes for one loss.

Lt. Hagarty—M.I.A.

*   *   *

May 19, 1944 #

Mission #20. Bomber Escort.

Today we had a light escort job, taking in 120 Forts below Paris, turning north and bombing an airfield there. We made landfall below Le Havre and made R/V at the same time. We then turned southeast until we were south of Paris where we turned north to Paris. The bombers hit the airport with very good results. All the bombs seemed to fall on the field and hangers. The bombers run into heavy flak over the target, and light flak at several other points.

There were an unusually large number of little friends in the area; due, I guess, to the large no of E/A encountered yesterday. No E/A sighted today.

Yesterday our Group saw about 4 gaggles (bunches) of E/A consisting of about 100+ E/A. Our Group destroyed twelve and damaged 6 with no losses. Good show!

* * *

May 21, 1944 #

Mission #21. Dive Bombing.

This is the first time we have had a dive bombing mission since I arrived on ops. We carried two 108 gal. wing tanks and a 500# Demolition Bomb on the belly. The bombs had an 8 to 11 second delayed action fuse to give us time to get safely away before the blast. Our targets were railway bridges in the edge of Happy Valley and railway sheds.

We made landfall above a 10/10 overcast and proceeded inland. We lost the rest of the Group when we climbed up through the clouds and went the entire trip alone. We were unable to find any holes to bomb through and finally bombed some flak emplacements on the way home. The rest of the group had better luck and bombed some locomotives and marshalling yards. Our squadron found eight locomotives in one area and damaged, probably destroying all of them. One engine was knocked off the track by one bomb. The three squadrons got around 15 locomotives in all. There were lots of other groups operating today and according to S2, over 200 locomotives were damaged in all.

We overshot the field coming home and landed at a Sterling base to find our way home. The clouds were down to 1500 ft and haze made it almost impossible to see the ground even then. We arrived back at the base about 30 minutes after the rest of the boys. We wouldn't have gotten lost except the leader's radio was out and we didn't know it in time to get a homing. Saw very moderate, inaccurate flak, but the rest ran into intense, accurate flak. Fourteen ships had flak hits in them, none serious.

* * *

May 22, 1944 #

Mission #22. Dive Bombing (Escort)

We almost had some bombs to carry today, but 8th Ftr. Command changed their minds the last minute and we were escort and top cover for the 84th who were carrying a 500 pounder on each wing, and a 108 gal belly tank, a load of over 2000# which is a lot for a fighter.

Our targets today were the three railway bridges over the Canal Edward east of Brussels. There were clouds at 5000 ft when we took off, and about the same over the target. We found a big hole and all of us went down and furnished top cover while the boys skip bombed. The results were fair, getting hits on the approaches to the bridge and one on the bridge. There were also many near misses that skipped past the bridges.

After the bombing we went in a few miles further hunting for locomos and targets of opportunity. Our flight leader would not go down lower than 3000 feet as he took it on himself to furnish top cover while the other boys shot up the engines. I was very P.O'ed as we had several good chances to put some of the Fuhrer's trains out of commission. However we withdrew after about 15 minutes after seeing them shoot up about 10 locomos and a power house.

We climbed back over the overcast and came on home. We ran into flak when we passed near Antwerp, and some accurate flak around the locomo but only two planes were damaged to any extent. Results were 12 locomotives damaged.

Dive bombing today was impossible due to the low clouds, thus the reasons for skip bombing, which was done at about 50 ft height.

* * *

May 25, 1944 †

Mission #23. Bomber Escort.

Today we were scheduled for a "to our limit" escort job with 8 boxes of Forts which were bombing Metz (where their flak almost got me on May 12th), and several other marshalling yards around western Germany. We made landfall near Le Havre and continued inland. We were using 108 gal wing tanks and could go at least five hours today. However, I had the sad misfortune to be in a flight with a pilot who was finishing his last mission today. His radio went out, so when the 4th and 56th Groups joined us, we came on home. We missed some action as our group got three 190s and shot up several locomotives. However we missed all the fun and only got about 3:30 while the other boys got about an hour longer.

Lt. Genge—M.I.A.

* * *

May 29, 1944 † † †

Mission # 24. Bomber escort.

Today we had a long hot mission up beyond Hanover. We were supposed to give close support to the lead box of bombers, but due to their being a few minutes early and spread out so far, we never did completely catch them. We made L/F at the southern end of the Frisian Islands and turned a little south. We began to pass the last box after about 30 minutes and continued east foward the front box. We passed the three boxes behind the first one but didn't have but very little time with the front of the formation before our time was up and we had to turn for home. Before we turned back we were relieved by Mustangs and P-38s. They were scheduled to take them (bombers) over the targets as our range wouldn't let us go the complete trip. We really expected some enemy planes today but they didn't show up. We came home across the Zuider Zee below Amsterdam and on home. An uneventful trip, though we had a couple of chances to go down on trains, it was Lt. Bernhart's last mission and he said he'd be damned if he'd get shot down on this last one down on the deck after a train.

Yesterday we lost three men in this most dangerous of all sports—strafing. Capt. Juckheim having 17 enemy planes to his credit, Lt. Hazlett, one of our squadron, and a darn good flight leader, and Lt. Orvis one of the new boys in our squadron. Capt. Juckheim and Lt. Hazzelett bailed out and what happened to Lt. Orvis no one knows.

Capt. Juckheim M.I.A.
Lt. Hazlett M.I.A.
Lt. Orvis N.Y.R.

*   *   *

May 31, 1944

Mission #25. Fighter Sweep.

The mission today was a "Type 16" Fighter sweep, with "GINFIZZ", an English Radar Station giving us courses to fly to find possible E/A. These boys are able to tell us when there are enemy planes up and their approximate altitude as far as a hundred miles inland from the enemy coast.

At briefing we were told by the weather officer that weather would be good, but we ran into towering cumulus clouds about 18,000 ft at the enemy coast and I lost my flight due to the thickness of the cloud. I wouldn't have lost them but the flight leader lost a lot of altitude and I continued climbing trying to get above the overcast. I flew on instruments for about 20 minutes in clouds so thick I could hardly see my wing tips before I finally broke out above the stuff. My flight leader had become lost and I found the squadron and joined another flight while my flight leader came on home.

We received one vector up to Charleroi to investigate some bogies in that area but we didn't see any E/A at all. We returned home after sweeping the area for about two hours. We passed out at Knocke, just a short way below the Hague in Holland. Very little flak was seen and it was directed toward some big friends coming out. This was a wing tank trip and we had plenty of gas and didn't have to worry about that item anyway.

*   *   *

June 2, 1944 # !

Mission #26.

Today was another double mission day and a very tiring one at that. Our first mission this morning was an area support fighter sweep. We were to give support in an area from La Troquet south to Rouen, east to Reims and north to Lille. We had as base altitude 20,000 ft. and most of this time were a little lower than this. There were about two other groups of P-47's and P-51's also in the area, and Fritz would have been crazy to come up with that many fighters around. About 900 heavy bombers were pounding coastal batteries, ack-ack installations and other defenses on the rocket coast from Calais to Le Treport but I don't know whether it was very successsful due to the overcast.

*   *   *

June 2, 1944 #

Mission #27

This is the second mission today and also was a fighter sweep, but with a little escort job coming out. We flew in as far as Reims at an altitude of 21,000 ft to keep any enemy fighters from molesting the bombers who were at this time bombing some airfields and marshalling yards south of Paris. Our object was to keep any E/A from being sent down there from the sector north of Reims. They probably knew better as their radar and spotter organizations keep them very well informed as to our strength and type of A/C (aircraft).

We turned southwest, at Reims and continued till we intercepted the bombers on their way home. They were running through flak, every few miles but weren't bothered by E/A. We gave them close escort and left a flight of 4 planes to get each straggler home. One plane (bomber) receved a direct hit from flak and burst into flames. Three chutes were seen to open before the bomber went in.

We escorted them practically across the Channel and turned for home. We landed at 10:30 and it was just getting dark. Got 6:55 today (time—combat).

* * *

June 3, 1944 [hand-drawn cross, "our worst loss to date"]

Mission #28.

And still another Type 16, Fighter Sweep over France, the third one in a row. The bombers, 240 Forts and 60 Libs, were still pounding the Rocket Coast around Calais down to Le Troquet. Our Group seemed to be the only one in our area and only one plane was sighted. No flak at all was seen and no nothing. This was a quieter mission than if we were back in Florida, and you could only tell there was a war going on by the smoking ports on the coast. We flew several vectors from "OILSKIN" our radar controller, and came home after about 2 hours

* * *

[hand-drawn cross] June 4, 1944

Lost Capt. Wilkinson on a local flight when he hit mountain in clouds. He was top ranking ace on the field with 10 destroyed, 13 damaged.

* * *

June 4, 1944 †

Mission #29

We had an early mission this morning and is the same type we have been having the past few days. We were giving area protection for the bombers that were beating up the coastal defenses from Calais south to Dieppe. There were about 5 Groups in the area and no E/A were sighted. They would have been crazy to try anything today with all the air power we had up.

Something must be going to pop soon as they are really softening up the Rocket coast more than they have in weeks. We came home between Calais and Dunkerque, encountering moderate accurate flak.

Yesterday Lt. Steinwedel failed to return from the mission. The third one of our boys from Marianna.

Lt. Steinwedel—N.Y.R.

* * *

June 4, 1944

Mission #30

This is the second mission today and is another Type 16 and area sweep. We had the area from Lille to Boulogne, to Le Troquet over to Rouen and back up to Lille. We were responsible to see that no E/A came through this area to molest the bombers who had quite a hard time as they had to bomb through an almost solid overcast. We saw some of the bombers when they plastered the port areas and left many fires. We encountered no E/A and no flak, either—unusual for this area.

* * *

June 6, 1944 # "D-Day"

Mission #31

Well, it has happened! Our first mission today was about daylight and we had breakfast at 4:00, which is too early. We are to give an area support in an area west of the beachhead. The actual invasion began last night about mid-night and has been going on regularly since. The Allies are using 4,000 ships and an umbrella of 5,000 planes to cover the invasion. About 12 Groups of Spits, and 40 Groups of P-38's are covering the beachhead and about 8 Groups of P-47s & 10 Groups of P-51's are giving area support around the area for 150 miles. Over 2000 heavy bombers are pounding the area from early this morning till tonite and our support has to be all day long from dawn till dark to keep out any enemy fighters. The Allies landed from Le Havre (British) to the Western end of the Cherbourg Peninsula (Americans). We gave area support for 4 hours and came on home. We saw innumerable bombers and quite a bit of flak, though most of it was directed at the bombers. Looks like quite a busy few days ahead. No E/A were sighted.

* * *

June 6, 1944 # D-Day

Mission #32

This is a continuation of our support to the invasion though we had to go to an area east of Amiens and carried bombs—250 pounders on each wing. And were looking for targets of opportunity. We were really trying to find some troop movements as there had been rumors of the 2nd Panzer Division moving from this area toward the beach-head. We found no traces of this movement however, and bombed some railroad yards, barges and shot up three locomotives.

We came home over Dunkerque and got plenty of reception. They don't seem to like for us to go over this area. Dicks almost got hit by the first bursts of flak, but took evasive action and came out okay.

* * *

June 6, 1944 # D-Day

Mission #33

We had the same area as on the early mission this morning and were to give protection to about 300 C-47s and the same number of gliders they were bringing onto the beach-head area. This type of aircraft is absolutely helpless and must have good support. None were lost to E/A either, though about 1% were knocked down by flak which is a very low percentage. They landed at 9:30 P.M. and we left the area soon afterward.

This is the third mission today and about 13 hours of flying. I am about as tired as a human can get and live. Getting to bed at 12:30 and breakfast at 4:00—not long to rest—I flew 13 combat hours today, and feel like I have done a day's work.

* * *

June 7, 1944 # † †

Mission #34

This morning we took off at 7:30 instead of 5:30 and I didn't mind that extra sleep. We had wing bombs and were scheduled to attack marshalling yards and convoys on the roads in the Lille sector. We have had awful weather the past two days and clouds everywhere. We were in the overcast practically all the way over there and stayed on top while the 84th went down to see how low the bases of the clouds were. They said for us to stay on top as the overcast was too low for bombing. However our flights became separated from the rest of the squadron and we flew east about twenty miles and found a big break in the clouds. We selected a double track railway bridge near a marshalling yard and dive bombed it—starting our dive in string at 8,000 ft and pulling out, releasing our bombs at 2,000 ft. We got at least four direct hits on the bridge destroying a big portion of the tracks.

The other bunch below the overcast ran into about 20#-109's and got two but lost two boys—Lts. Just and Rice. They left the area about the time we did and all the rest returned safely. We (our flight) got a little flak when we hit the bridge. Lt. Wilkinson and Lt. Slater hit in the leg by 20mm fragment of flak—not serious.

Lt. Just & Lt. Rice—M.I.A.

*   *   *

June 7, 1944

Mission #35.

This is the second mission today and we have an entirely new area for our group. We also have frag. cluster bombs. These clusters have six-20# bombs on each wing and when they explode the fragments have a velocity of about 3300 ft. per second—faster than an army rifle.

We were giving support to a Task Force of Forts who were bombing an airport on the bottom of the Brest Peninsula. We watched them bomb and they gave the dispersal area around the field a good pounding, then we dive bombed the field with our frag. bombs, all of them seemingly hitting in the target area.

We continued out behind the bombers and arrived home with no losses or damaged planes.

*   *   *

June 8, 1944

Mission #36.

This was my only mission today as they let me sleep this morning due to my having flown every mission since the invasion started. We had wing bombs today and were to hit targets of opportunity in area south of Amiens. Some of the boys bombed an air field and our flight hit marshalling yards loaded with tank and box cars. My flight leader overshot, but my two bombs lifted a couple of cars up into the air. We then turned around and strafed the tank cars, and I noticed many hits on them. They were empty however as we didn't start any fires. We continued across and turned to make a second pass and ran into some heavy 20mm flak from the ground west of the tracks. We took evasive action and shot up the cars a second time. We then located some barges on a canal and gave them a good burst. By this time most everyone had gone home. Lundegrin, my flight leader and I continued home alone as our #3 & #4 man had become separated from us. Luckily no Huns saw us as we would have been duck soup for a 1/2 dozen or so of them. We landed after everyone else had got home about 30 minutes. I fired 800 rounds and not many were wasted.

*   *   *

June 10, 1944 † † † †

Mission #37

Today we had three missions and I flew them all. The first one we had the area above Rouen to work over with bombs and strafing. We went in at St. Valery and continued to our area before we let down through the overcast. We shot up a couple of trains, several trucks (army) and other targets we bombed. We lost Lt. Kuehner when he hit a tree on a bombing run and he crashed, his bombs exploding—He didn't have a chance to get out. Lt. Baker, Lt. Loyd, and Lt. McIntosh are also missing from this mission.

Lt. Kuehner—K.I.A.
Lt. Baker, Lt. Loyd, Lt. McIntosh—M.I.A.

*   *   *

June 10, 1944

Mission #38

Just after lunch time (we didn't have a chance to eat) we got a notice from 8th FTR Command for a "rush" mission. The Fourth Group had reported two troop trains on the Brest Peninsula proceeding toward the beach-head and we needed 8 men for the mission. We had to go the 50 miles over the water at 300 ft. so that their radar wouldn't pick us up and so they wouldn't know we were coming. We got in before they knew it but couldn't find the trains anywhere—thought we did shoot up one engine on a siding. We bombed a railroad bridge with 2—500# delayed action bombs per plane but did very little damage.

We returned to the Channel on the deck and climbed up to 2,000 ft and came on home.

*   *   *

June 10, 1944 † † † † † †

Mission #39

This is the third bombing mission today and was in the same area as in the first mission today. We had two 250# delayed action bombs and located some marshalling yards to lay them in. We were supposed to bomb an ammo dump but couldn't find it. I laid my two bombs along side the box cars and blew about half a dozen off the track with the two bombs. We looked around for something to shoot up but couldn't find anything else. On mission at noon today we lost five men from 83rd sqdn due to enemy fighters.

M.I.A.—Maj. Stump, Maj. McLeod, Capt. Hunt, Lt. Casey (1st Lt), Lt. Lacey

Lt. McDermott killed in crash when he and his wingman hit in overcast.

June 10, 1944

As a short summary for today, I would like to explain the loss of eleven pilots in one day. Lt. Kuehner crashed while bombing, Lt. Baker failed to return—was last seen by himself. Lt. Loyd, Lt. McIntosh of 84th were shot down by flak. Major Stump, Major McLeod, Capt. Hunt, Lt. Casey and Lt. Lacey were last heard from when they were heard to say that they were being jumped by a bunch of M.E. 109's. Lt. McDermott and another pilot ran together on the climb out on a mission and Lt. McDermott was killed, and the other fellow bailed out—breaking his ankle and getting pretty badly shaken up. This is by far the worst day the Group has had since it was formed over a year ago. If I live through this tour, I'll really be surprised. & Lucky.

*   *   *

June 11, 1944 # †

Mission #40

Today we continued with our bombing missions against marshalling yards and convoys (on the roads). We had two 100# instantaneous bombs and some of the fellows had 2—250# delayed action bombs. We were still operating in the Amiens area, as we have in the past couple of days.

We crossed in at St. Valery and continued south to about 50 miles below Amiens where we dive bombed a big marshalling yards with only fair results. We also went down to look for transportation on the roads, but all we saw were a couple of engines and they were quickly polished off. Some goods wagons (box cars) were also strafed before we returned home. We still are having very bad weather over the Continent and England—since the invasion started the weather has been P.P.

(Lt. Casey (2nd Lt)—M.I.A.)

*   *   *

June 13, 1944 # †

Mission #41.

From all indications we might as well have gotten into a bombardment squadron, as we have been on dive, skip, and glide bombing missions regularly since the evening of "D" day.

Today we had a railroad bridge to dive bomb and put out of commission. It was located southwest of Paris about 50 miles and we were using 2—500# instantaneous bombs to do the job. On the way out we flew good compact formation and this alone saved us from being bounced by about 30# Huns just below Rouen. They circled out about five miles from us and looked for some flight to get behind but after losing those 10 men the other day—we are a damn sight more careful.

The target was covered at 10,000 ft. with a thin layer of clouds and we dive bombed from 10 to 3 thousand feet before releasing the bomb. My first pass wasn't good so I went around and glide bombed from 5 down to 1 thousand ft. A couple of 20mm flak emplacements got me in their crossfire but luckily I got out okay. My bombs went a little to the left of target.

Coming back the weather over England was terrible and visibility down to about 300 ft. I landed at a field a few miles from ours and caught a ride on into Duxford. Went back this evening and got the plane.

Capt. Ramsey was killed instantly yesterday on his first mission by a direct hit by heavy flak. He had my plane. The entire plane burst into flames and crashed with apparently no one getting out.

*   *   *

June 14, 1944 #

Mission #42

For a nice change we had a bomber escort mission instead of a dive bombing mission. We were escorting part of a force of 1500 bombers who were blasting airfields in Belgium, Holland, France and Germany. This makes me so happy as the G.A.F. have concentrated about 500 single engine E/A in the western France area. These boys won't bother us as long as we are together but woe be it to a fight who becomes separated—they've "had it".

We escorted several boxes of bombers across airfields in the Brussels area. The radar controller reported bandits in our area at one time but no contact was made with them.

I was flying a new P-47 model D-25 which has a souped up engine, a full paddle-blade hydromatic prop and a blister canopy. These are beautiful ships and fly good. Visibility is very good and it is quite an improvement over the other ships. I have been flying this ship since my plane was lost a couple of days ago. My new plane that is assigned to me is also a D-25 and should be ready for combat in a couple of days.

I returned home a little early as my receiver was out on "A" channel.

*   *   *

June 14, 1944 # !

Mission #43

This is the second mission today and we're back in the groove with two—500# on each wing again. This was a rather unusual mission as we were to bomb a pinpoint target below the Amiens area. The target was a building which controls all German A/C in this area and was very important.

We had calls all the way in to the target from the controller who warned us of E/A in several areas near our target but none were seen as we all stuck together and gave each other top cover as each squadron bombed. The Huns have a dirty habit of bouncing us below the clouds when we are concentrating on the target and we have to have a squadron on top for top cover to keep this from taking place. We had to bomb through clouds and there were very few hits in the target area. I pulled up after my bombing run from 12 down to 4,000 ft and ran through about ten acres of 20mm flak exploding all around me. This is some of the heaviest light flak I have seen. We also got some heavy flak over all A/D that we circled over near the target. Only one plane was damaged by flak though it's a wonder someone didn't get it there.

We returned over Cayaux and collected some heavy flak at Criel on the way out. We landed at 10:00 and its was still an hour before dark—long days here in the E.T.O.

Radio again went out on "A" channel—must have it checked closely.

*   *   *

This is my half way point on my tour. I now have about 150 hours.

June 16, 1944

Mission #44.

Today we had another of those too, too few escort missions that we have seen very little of lately. We were standing by all this morning as our first mission was scrubbed just after we had our briefing.

We are still having bad weather and had to climb out through two overcasts as there were two layers of clouds we had to get through to reach our base altitude. These overcasts are pretty bad at times and it is very easy to get vertigo or (the feeling you have when you are in a cloud. You feel like you are up in a bank and turning when really you are flying straight and level.)

We were a little ahead of the bombers and didn't meet them till they were making their bombing run on their target which was an A/D south west of Paris.

The 83rd & 84th Squadrons went on out with the bombers while our squadron stayed around and tried to find some targets of opportunity. There was nothing found however except a couple of cars and the first flight shot them up. I had better explain that the only persons in a car in France are either Germans or people working for the Germans, so we don't have to worry about hurting some Frenchman.

We collected some flak, light and heavy near an air field but no one was hit and we came on home without further excitement.

*   *   *

June 17, 1944

Mission #45.

Things are getting better as far as I'm concerned—we had two bomber escort missions today and according to Col. Gray we will have lot more of them instead of so many dive bombing missions. This is what we are really trained to do, as the Ninth Air Force Thunderbolts are the fighter-bomber boys.

On the first mission I flew on Col. Gray's wing as Surtax white two. To explain our line-up system—Each squadron has a call sign—ours is Surtax—the 83rd is Cargo, the 84th is Shampoo. Each squadron has four flights with four planes per fight; the Flights are named after colors—the first flight is white, the second is red, 3rd is yellow and the last flight is blue flight. Therefore our Group has 48 planes to go on each mission.

We made R/V with our box of bombers just after they had bombed and escorted them back all the way to the English coast. We couldn't get too near as those boys are awfully trigger-happy and shoot at anything. Once in a while we have to call on "C" channel and tell them we will leave them if they don't get on the ball.

Major Gilbert and his flight went down below the clouds to observe the bombing results and ran into a flight of 5 F.W. 190's. They were so surprised and scared that two of the 190's crashed trying to get away—without being fired at.

*   *   *

June 17, 1944

Mission #46

This is the second mission we have had today and they were both escort jobs. On our way out, the radar controller called us and said to be on the look-out for a "diver" which is his name for the radio controlled pilotless planes (rocket-propelled) that the Germans have been sending over. We were to shoot the thing down if we saw it—but not get nearer than 600 yards as the blast effect from them is dangerous any nearer. However, we saw nothing and continued south, crossing out at Beachy Head and made landfall for the first time at the beachhead, and saw several of the towns they have been fighting for the past few days.

We found our two boxes of bombers and stayed with them while they bombed. I have never seen so many bombers and fighters this close to the coast. There were lots of B-17s, B-24s, B-26s, A-20s, P-38s, P-47s and P-51s in the area and there wasn't a chance of seeing any enemy fighters with all this air power.

We saw a bunch of boats at the beach head while passing over and things looked pretty busy down there. However they were 20,000 ft. below us, so we couldn't tell too much about it.

We came out with our bombers and left them just above Le Havre and crossed back in at Beachy Head. The R.A.F. had a couple of flights of Spits up looking us over when we crossed in and I'm glad to see they're "on the ball."

* * *

June 20, 1944 # * !

Mission #47.

This morning we had a short escort mission and area support at the same time. We were to receive our directions from the controller "Oilskin" after we had entered our area. We were awakened at 3:30, ate breakfast and had briefing at 4:20 with take-off at 5:05. We arrived in our area about 6:30 and began to fly a rectangular course over the area we were to patrol. We continued at this for about 30 minutes and then picked up a small box of bombers and gave them support.

While we were with the bombers we noticed contrails high and to our left. They were flying no formation at all and looked suspiciously like Huns. We shoved everything forward (gave it more power) and started climbing up. The bogies turned out to be 20# ME 109s and they also started to climb as soon as they saw we were coming after them. Our first two flights made contact with them about 30 to 32 thousand ft and went into a Luftbury with them. Two of the E/A made a bounce on Hosford and he broke violently left, did a couple of snap rolls and lost the E/A.

However his wing man failed to return from the mission, though no one saw him go down. He could have gone down when the two E/A bounced them.

The E/A finally split S for the deck and we followed them down but lost them in the overcast. Capt. Mayo got one going straight down and he crashed making over 500 mph. Those boys had more altitude, cloud cover above and below them and every advantage but we gave them an aggressive fight.

Lt. Hodges—N.Y.R.

*   *   *

June 20, 1944 #

Mission #48

This evening we had a dive bombing mission back in our old area below Amiens. We had some "gin" from higher up that the 2nd Panzer Div was moving down through this area on about 80 trains and these were to be our targets.

We followed two main railroads that ran from Amiens to Paris and were on the lookout for any of these troop movements. However none were found and the three squadrons dive bombed about six marshalling yards with better than usual results. Our flight hit a yard that had about 30 or 40 boxcars in it and got about 6 or 8 hits from our 250# bombs in the target area, destroying several boxcars and cutting the tracks. We started our dive at 8,000 ft. and released our bombs at about 2,000 ft. One of my bombs hit on a loading platform with no visible damage and the other bomb destroyed two boxcars and a short stretch of track.

We were pretty low on gas so we didn't do any strafing—though we had some pretty good targets with apparently very little ground fire to bother us. We ran into some heavy flak over some A/D's but that was about all. No E/A were seen by any of the three squadrons.

Hours to go—133:00

*   *   *

June 21, 1944   128:00 hrs to go

Mission #49

This morning we had a long mission escorting about 1500 heavy bombers on the largest daylight raid of the war. A group of the 9th Air Force came up and stayed here overnight to help with the support on this big raid.

We took off early as we always do on a bomber mission and made R/V with the bombers over the overcast about the enemy coast and continued inland with our six boxes. We were a little late so we had to run a little faster to make the time up. We hit several points where the flak was heavy but no one was damaged. We left the bombers a little northeast of Hanover and came on home. We passed many little friends going in to give the bomber withdrawal support. No E/A sighted.

Was put in for D.F.C. yesterday.

* * *

June 21, 1944   124:00 to go

Mission #50

This evening we had a Type 16 area support mission while three boxes of bombers were hitting A/D's and other "no ball" targets around the Pas De Calais area. We were vectored to several points but encountered no E/A nor even sighted any.

After the bombers had finished their mission and left the area we were to look for targets of opportunity such as trains, marshalling yards and truck convoys. We saw nothing in this area moving so we finally strafed a marshalling yard and some barges on a canal near the yards. After this was done we were all low on gas and continued home. A couple or four of the fellows had flak hits but none serious. All these were from light ground fire. My flight leader was hit just ahead of me but I didn't receive a scratch.

* * *

June 22, 1944 # †   120:00 to go!

Mission #51

This mission is one from which I was lucky to return. We had another Type 16 and area support mission for the first hour and after the bombers left we were to look for targets of opportunity and we hit on an area where there was plenty of activity. Our flight went over a town and I happened to see a locomotive and our squadron leader said if I saw one for our flight to go down after it and they would give us top cover. My flight leader didn't see them so he told me to lead them down.

We found two trains and on the first pass we shot up the engine, on the second pass we shot up and set fire to a flak car on the end of the train—killing about everyone of the gun crews. On this pass I cut the top four cables on a high tension line running by the track. I knocked off my pilot tube (from which my air speed operates) and cut a deep gash in my wing and making dents in my prop and other wing. We then shot up the other engine, turned around and dive bombed the first train, scoring several good direct hits.

We left this area and a little further south found a double header and made three passes and knocked out both engines. Hosford shot up the middle of the train and hit some ammunition cars, exploding four cars and tearing up the track and about half the train. Luckily he was a good ways off and he and his wingman received only slight damage from the flying pieces of the train.

By this time we had to come home because of gas but our four ships did okay—four locomotives, two flak cars, and about half of two trains destroyed. (My plane is in hangar for repairs).

1Lt. Gibbs—Killed in action.

*   *   *

June 23, 1944

Mission #52

This evening we had a rush mission that was split between escort and divebombing. We picked up six boxes of Libs that were bombing some airfields and escorted them from the Cherbourg Peninsula into the target area and then left them with another group that came in to relieve us.

We turned north and hunted up a marshalling yard that had been reported as having a train loaded with oil cars. When we arrived they were gone, however and we dive bombed the yards, cutting the tracks at several points and damaging some repair buildings. The 83rd found a train loaded with trucks and left the locomotive and train burning fiercely, and it was a beautiful sight. No E/A were seen and very little flak.

*   *   *

June 24, 1944   114:00 to go

Mission #53

This really shouldn't be called a mission but since it was over the beachhead we were told to log combat time. We were picked to fly a couple of generals down to the beach head or rather to give them comforting escort so they would feel safe. Lt. Young, Lt. Scholtz and I had the mission and didn't even land while there. We flew above the two major generals all the way there, circled the landing strip till they had landed then returned home. All this was, to say the least, a waste of time.

*   *   *

July 1, 1944 # * !

Mission #54

I have two people or one person and God to thank for being back after this mission. It is by far my closest call and if these incidents aren't repeated, I'll truly be happy. To begin with, we had 2-250# bombs on each wing and a bad cross wind for takeoff. Two of the first eight ships that took off collided and crashed about a quarter of a mile from the field with a big explosion and fire, killing both pilots instantly. We took off over the burning wrecks and didn't feel good about it. I went to a crash a fews days ago and saw what was left of the pilot and it's an awful sight.

We climbed through three layers of clouds and proceeded southeast toward our target which was a canal and some locks and barges.

Our radar controller notified us that there were bandits at 23,000 ft. at point H which our code for this trip was St. Quentin. We were about in this area at 12,000 feet when the first bandits were seen very high and seemed to be preparing to attack. About half a minute later I saw five ME-109s coming in behind me about 300 yards. I called for my flight to break left and broke left myself. I saw that they still were able to hit me and tried an old stunt Hosford had got away with on an occasion very similar to mine. I pulled the stick back in my belly and kicked bottom rudder going into a violent spin to the left. There isn't a pilot living that can hit a guy in a spin and when I recovered, about 3,000 feet below where I started, I didn't have any elevator trim tab control. No E/A either. I surmised that a hit had severed the cable and had to keep a lot of forward pressure on the stick to fly straight and level.

We stayed in the area about 15 minutes and weren't able to find any other E/A. They had made attacks on three other flights at the same time they made their attack on my flight. Lt. Landigan was hit and also received wounds in the hands, Lt. Sharpe is at a hospital near here, his condition unknown and Lt. Orr of the 83rd was shot down. Three E/A were destroyed and we are darn lucky that the Lord looked after the rest of us.

I received two 20mm cannon shells in my tail surface and was darn lucky my controls weren't completely gone. My plane will now have to go to the hangar again.

†-Lt. Kitley
†-Lt. Reese
†-Lt. Orr

*   *   *

Heard today that Lt. Roberts is P.O.W. Good news!

July 4, 1944 † # Independence (?) Day

Mission #55

This mission was an area support mission, our job being to take care of any bombers coming through our area. We had four boxes of bombers hitting airfields around Paris and gave them support while around the Paris area.

Our radar controller was really "on the ball" this morning and once he told us that he saw us over point "L" which was Paris. We looked down through the haze and there was Paris just below us. About this time they began to shoot up some fireworks to celebrate the 4th and we had to get out of there.

Lt. Moseley's engine froze up caused by lack of oil (probably) and he told us good-bye and jumped out. Otherwise there was very little unusual that happened. No E/A were seen.

Lt. Moseley M.I.A.

* * *

July 5, 1944 # †   103:50 to go

Mission #56

This was a long mission down south east of Tours and our job was bomber withdrawal. There were two boxes of B-17s on their way home from Italy after bombing some target on the Riviera. These are the same boys who were on the shuttle run across from England to Russia, to Italy and back. There were originally 140 of them and only 60 are coming home. Don't know where the rest are.

We climbed out through heavy clouds and broke out at about 5,500 ft. I was a little nervous as I just did get off with the wing tanks and the old plane I was using. I had to use water injection and my wheels just cleared the revetments at the end of the field. My plane is in the hangar still, due to the new tail not trimming correctly while flying. They also are giving it a paint job.

We crossed in Le Triport and continued on a course of 192 degrees for about an hour before we located the bombers. The 56th Group was with us and were also to give close support. About this time Surtax yellow 2 called and said his oil pressure was below 50 pounds sq/in and was going home. Yellow 4 went back and they got a homing to "Sweepstake" a homing station in Normandy (beachhead). On the way, they turned into some Spits that bounced them and yellow 4 lost Miller who was having the engine trouble and didn't see him again. He is at present N.Y.R. (Miller bailed out at beach head—safe).

We came on out with the bombers and saw no E/A though part of the group ran across a few 109's and 190's, but they escaped into the overcast.

Lt. Mullins—M.I.A.

*   *   *

July 6, 1944 #

Mission #57

This was the kind of mission that is good on your nerves. We sighted no E/A, and the flak was the only thing that kept us reminded of the war. We were also practicing a new type formation and it worked out well.

This was a Type 16, bomber escort and area support, our area being east of Calais and south to the Amiens area. We saw the bombers hit a couple of A/D's and and the results looked good. Visibility was excellent and we could see for at least a 100 miles. Below is a typical schedule, and the one used on this mission.

Takeoff 6:44
Set course 6:56
Bombers call name on "C" channel was "Vinegrove"
Bradwell Bay—142°—7:10
Furnes————144°—7:36
Lens—————182°—7:50
Lv. Furnes Area———9:00
Home————306°—9:27
checkpoints
s/Cambrai
t/Reims
r/Beauvais
i/Paris
n/Le Mans
g/Evreux
e/Saumur
y/Orleans

*   *   *

July 7, 1944 #

Mission #58

This was a long escort job and the kind we have seen too few of lately. There were about a 1000 Libs and Forts hitting aircraft factories and oil refineries at Leipzig and a couple of other points. We escorted the bombers from the Zuider Zee to Dummer Lake and then turned a little north on a fighter sweep ahead of the bombers, to try to find some enemy planes. None were seen by our group and we started on home at about 9:30 and shot up several locomotives on the way home. Two groups ran into some E/A a little after we left—just our luck. According to the combat report this evening, our fighters in the 8th Air Force got 75 E/A for a loss of only 6—good show.

*   *   *

July 9, 1944 #

Mission #59

This mission was at a very early part of the day and too early to suit me. They woke us at 3:30 to get up and eat breakfast, had briefing at 4:20 and takeoff was at 5:05. Due to the overcast over the base, it was still dark when we took off.

We were on a Type 16 patrol in the area just north of Paris and were in the area for about an hour and a half. We sighted several locomotives but didn't go down as we were on the lookout for E/A taking off and any that might be up after bombers in the area. No E/A were seen and we came on home without any trouble except a little flak north of Paris. Lt. Summer's plane had an engine quit and bailed out about 18 miles from the English coast. Air Sea Rescue launches picked him up and he is okay.

*   *   *

July 12, 1944 #

Mission #60

Today we gave close support to two Task Forces of Forts and Libs who were out to bomb Munich. We took off and climbed up through the grandfather of all overcasts. It extended from here to the target without a break in the clouds. The bombers had to bomb by radar, as they couldn't see the target, and the results were not known by us.

We picked them up south east of the Walcheren Islands and continued along with them to Saarbrucken where a couple of other groups of P-51s relieved us.

We brought a couple of stragglers home and made sure they made it okay. One bomber blew up in mid-air and knocked down another bomber. We went back to check for chutes but saw none. May be some of the boys got out below the clouds. No E/A seen but plenty of flak.

* * *

July 13, 1944 #

Mission #61

This is the third day in succession that the bombers have gone out to hit Munich, and our job today was the same as yesterday. We had a little more cloud than on yesterday's mission and the Group was pretty well split up till we made R/V about 20 miles west of Brussels.

We flew back and forth protecting the bombers and none of the last five boxes were bothered by E/A as long as we were with them. We went a little further than usual with them today and turned home after being relieved by other groups. This was an uneventful mission but I don't mind having about twenty more just like it. There was heavy intense flak at Saarbrucken and a little at other points.

* * *

July 14, 1944 #

Mission #62

Today we had a long and rather unusual mission. At briefing we were told that the bombers were to go down to 300 ft. to bomb instead of 20,000 ft, and the reason no one was sure of. Our S2 (Intelligence) section said the place was in a mountainous territory and said that they were probably dropping supplies to the French partisans.

We escorted the bombers from the Channel to within a few miles of the target where we were relieved by a P-51 Group. Blue flight shot up a locomotive on the way home, but otherwise it was a very quiet mission. Very little flak was seen and no E/A were seen by any of the Group.

Heard a nasty rumor today that we will soon be flying P-51s as they are going to change our Group from T-Bolts to P-51s.

* * *

July 16, 1944 #   75:00 more!

Mission #63

Believe it or not, the bombers again paid a visit to Munich, and Saarbrucken. They really must have something special down there to continue pounding there so regularly. We made R/V southwest of Brussels and continued in with the six boxes of the 1st Task Force. One of the Shampoo Squadron (84th) saw a plane go down in flames and they also saw a fight going on, so they went down to get in the fight but it was all over when they got down.

We continued with our bombers who turned south and bombed Saarbrucken, running through intense flak on the bombing run. However we saw none go down and as far as we could tell they all got back okay. We left them about fifty miles in the enemy coast and continued home. Only one E/A seen but plenty of flak.

*   *   *

July 19, 1944 # * † †

Mission #64

This mission is the longest one that I have been on thus far. I logged 5:10, which was time from takeoff to landing. We were on bomber escort and really don't believe we ever got with the bunch we were supposed to escort. However, we made R/V with a bunch of Libs a little below Antwerp and started toward the front boxes which were stretched out ahead. There were only about 1500 heavies in all and we reached almost to the first box before our time was up and we were to turn home.

About the time the P-51's relieved us we sighted three A/D below us and there were several airplanes on the two of them and none on the other. My flight, Surtax Red Flight, and the boys who couldn't release their wing tanks stayed up at 12,000 ft for top cover and some of the others went down on the A/D's. We lost our squadron C.O. from ground fire, as he crashed and burned on the edge of the field without a chance of getting out. Several others received small hits but no one else was lost. This was Major Munson's fourth mission since he returned from the U.S. from his furlough. He had already finished one tour and returned to fly another.

Our Group destroyed three E/A on one field and nine on the other. They all burned and made a pretty picture, each one sending up a pillar of black smoke. After the strafing we came on home, but were too far south of course, due to strong winds that we didn't know about. We also lost Capt. Lay yesterday when he bailed out after being hit by ground fire while strafing a train.

Capt. Lay—M.I.A.
Maj. Munson—K.I.A

*   *   *

July 19, 1944 † †

This evening we had one of the worst crashes here I have heard of in a long time. A Flying Fortress came in to the field to see two of the pilots here, as they were friends of theirs back in the States. They said they would give them a ride around the field in the Fort while they were here.

Two pilots from the 84th and two enlisted men from this field got in with them and they took off and buzzed the tower, but when they pulled up over the hangar their left wing hit a beacon light on top of the hangar and tore about twenty feet off the wing. This piece hit on the officers club and tore a big place in the roof. The Fort turned over on its back and crashed about 50 yards from my window against one of the big brick barracks where the 82nd Squadron enlisted men live.

I was about half asleep when it hit, exploded and began to burn viciously. I jumped up and was almost paralyzed by the sight and was almost sick on my stomach. I stayed back as the ammunition was going off and I was afraid of being hit. They got a bunch of fire trucks here but almost every thing was completely consumed before they could do a thing. I went up and watched them carry off what was left of the 14 men and it was awful. The big barracks was burned up and one man found in it, bring to a total of 15 men killed and about a million dollars in damages.

Even now, with everything cleaned up, I keep glancing out there to see if it wasn't just a horrible nightmare.

Lt. Smith—Killed in crash—he only had six or eight hours more on his tour
Lt. Putnam—Killed in crash.

*   *   *

July 21, 1944 #

Mission #65

More and more nice long escort jobs, and do I love them. I wouldn't care if all the rest of my combat flying was bomber escort. Today we ran a split mission—having the Group divided into two separate sections, with the "A" section taking off a little earlier than we did and their job was to protect the front boxes of bombers.

Our job was to protect the last six boxes, which were B-17s. When a force of 1200 bombers go out, they have about 20 boxes (60 per box) and strung out about 100 miles, so the Groups must also spread out this far and also in front and behind to ward off attacks by E/A.

We made R/V at the southern end of the Walcheren Islands over Flushing and made a couple of orbits (360° turn) before our boxes of bombers came along.

We gave them close support for about an hour thirty minutes before our time was up. They ran into heavy flak near Cologne and one bomber exploded in mid-air, knocking down another Fort near it. No chutes were seen and the second Fort fell apart and burned just before it reached the ground.

After turning back we found a marshalling yard and our three flights damaged (shot them fulla holes) six locomotives and strafed the cars. We then came out without anything further happening. Lt. Hosford got a couple of hits from flak but made it home okay.

All locomotives are listed as damaged unless they blow all to pieces, and when strafed they only have to change boilers and steam pipe and such.

* * *

July 24, 1944

Mission #66

Today we were giving area support to about 1200 heavies who were bombing the German strong points below St. Lo, on the right flank of the beach head. Our area was from St. Malo to Vire and north to about 20 miles south of Paris. Our job as usual was to intercept any E/A so they wouldn't get to the bombers.

We swept the area that was given us and after the bombers left we went down on the deck looking for any transportation on the move, but didn't see anything so we came on home.

No E/A seen and no flak directed at us—unusually quiet. One group of P-51s reported contacting some E/A near Evreaux and a few claims were made

* * *

July 25, 1944

Mission #67

Today we are back in about the same area as yesterday and doing the same job. It seems that the bombers didn't bomb yesterday due to the overcast and are giving it a try today again. Our area has moved over a little and we are to give support from St. Malo west on the Brest Peninsula.

We were on instruments for almost an hour and finally had to let back down from 25,000 ft to 12,000 ft before it was clear. We then patrolled up and down the Brest Peninsula looking for ground targets and E/A. No E/A was seen but the colonel and his flight shot up some goods wagons and marshalling yards. They picked up some flak but all made it back home. No heavy flak only 20mm and machine gun fire.

* * *

July 28, 1944 †

Mission #68

Today we gave area support and protection for some Big Friends bombing airfields in the Paris area. After crossing in the French coast at Fecamp we proceeded to Evreux and flew around looking for enemy planes. The only enemy we saw was a good bit of heavy accurate flak from gun positions on the Seine River northwest of Paris. We turned south, making a course down around Paris and then headed north. We continued north and came out at the Walcheren Islands in Holland. Due to there being a solid overcast we saw the ground only a few times. We saw other Little Friends in the area, as some were on an escort job to Leipzig.

Lt. Morris—Killed while strafing some trucks; crashed into small forest—

* * *

July 29, 1944

Mission #69

Our bombers, 60-Lbs, went down north of Paris, still after airfields in this area. On the climb out we went through an overcast about 8,000 ft. thick and it was filled with snow. We picked up our bombers at the English coast and escorted them over the entire trip, and gave them extremely good protection. We stayed with the Big Friends till they crossed out at Flushing. We found bad weather back at the base with very low clouds, mist and haze, and were all glad when we got back on the ground.

* * *

July 30, 1944

Mission #70

This afternoon we had another area patrol (fighter sweep) with takeoff at 4:15. I was flying in Capt. Woller's flight and this was his last mission. We had to fly through some towering cumulus clouds on the climb out and everyone lost their leader and had to continue through alone on instruments. We got together again when we got on top and the Group reformed. We had good weather over France and could see the ground most of the time. We received several vectors from "oilskin" (our radar controller) but they all turned out to be Little Friends in the area. We went down to 8,000 feet and gave top cover to Red Flight while they shot up some trains. We then went down ourselves and found a locomotive which we polished off.

We ran into heavy, bad clouds over the channel, but it was better back home over the base. Major Eby and Lt. Fitzgerald both received hits in their canopy and in each instance the shells hit the bullet proof glass and glanced away, thereby saving their lives.

* * *

July 31, 1944

Mission #71

This mission today was a very long escort job. Our job was to give support to six boxes of Forts in the 3rd Air Task Force on withdrawal from Munich. On our way out we ran into some very accurate flak that followed us around like our shadow. Those boys are plenty good at throwing up that stuff. We made R/V with the bombers north east of Saarbrucken and continued to the rear of the boxes. Due to their having plenty of support we swept the area behind them on the way out but no E/A were seen. Cargo (83rd) Blue Flight went down and strafed an A/D, destroying three planes and one of their boys, Lt. Korsemeyer, had his engine shot out and had to bail out.

We continued home behind the bombers and left them a little inside the English coast.

* * *

August 3, 1944 # †

Mission #72

This mission was a dive-bombing-strafing affair and was in the Beauvois area, which is a warm part of France and I don't mean the climate. I was flying as element leader in our squadron c.o.'s flight on this mission.

We arrived in our area about 5:15 and Capt. Clark picked out a small innocent marshalling yards and went down to glide bomb it. Capt. Clark was first across it, his wing man next, I was next and my wing man last. Capt. Clark received a hit in his engine and we stayed with him till his engine quit and watched him bail out and land safely. As we were then separated from our squadron we climbed up to 12,000 ft and came home. We got a couple of good hits on the marshalling yards.

Capt. Clark—M.I.A.

*   *   *

August 4, 1944

Mission #73

This morning we took off a little after lunch on another bombing and strafing mission. Our area today was the area between Saarbrucken and Metz. I had a 250 pound bomb under each wing and a 165 gal. belly tank as our area is about 350 miles from here and would require a lot of gas.

We arrived in our area okay and the Group split up, each squadron selecting their own targets. We selected a large marshalling yard and our squadron did a good job of bombing. We had all but about three of the bombs hit in the area, destroying the tracks and goods wagons.

We looked for locomotives and targets such as trucks, but couldn't find a thing moving. We then climbed up and came home.

Saw one Fort go down and about 10 chutes, so I guess everyone got out.

*   *   *

August 5, 1944

Mission #74

This mission was one of the long hard kind, hard on your nerves and the seat of your pants. We were giving the first two boxes penetration and target support while they bombed oil refineries and aircraft factories at Hamburg.

We picked up our bombers southwest of Bremen after going all the way over water, skirting the Frisian Islands. Our bombers turned inland before they reached Hamburg and received a lot of flak when they crossed in. We continued along with them as they reached the target and here they received a lot of flak. Saw three bombers go down, one exploding at about 20,000 ft. The 56th came in about this time and we started home.

Part of our boys brought home some stragglers so they could give their location to S2 in case they had to ditch in the Channel. We lost no one today and may we have more days like it.

*   *   *

August 6, 1944 # * †

Mission #75

Finally—!! I got me a ME—109 destroyed in the air—We were on target support and withdrawal for about 1200 heavies that were hitting Hamburg's docks and an oil storage dump. We reached the area just as the first boxes were bombing and continued around southeast while the other boxes bombed. While there, Oilskin reported bandits in our area and we started looking for them. We saw contrails going toward the bombers and started climbing up to find out what they were. They turned out to be 8 ME-109's and they soon realized we were after them. They continued climbing and every couple of minutes two would split S for the deck. We couldn't follow as the others wuld then follow us. Finally we followed the last 2 down to 5,000 ft from 33,000 ft and went into a Luftbury. We couldn't turn inside them but finally I got on one's tail and gave him a long burst, which hit his left wing and in the cockpit. The wheels dropped down and his engine started burning before I overshot him. He went into a dive and I got a picture of him hitting the ground.

We then came on home at a low R.P.M. as we were all short on gas. The Group lost one man who bailed out on account of engine trouble. We also lost Lt. Myler in yesterday's mission.

Lt. Cummings—M.I.A. 8/6/44
Lt. Myler—K.I.A. 8/5/44

*   *   *

August 7, 1944

Mission #76

This was a miserable mission due to the weather and plenty of flak. We had 2— 250 pound G.P. Bombs and were out to hit any transportation in the area just south east of Paris. The haze was so bad we flew over several "hot spots" (heavy flak guns concentration) and were lucky we all got home. One boy had a 88 mm. shell go through his wing and luckily didn't explode or he wouldn't have been back.

We bombed a double track railroad loaded with boxcars and received several good hits on them. Due to the haze we didn't strafe any and continued home. We saw what we thought may have been an E/A but it disappeared in the clouds. Some of the other flights found several locomotives and trucks and shot them up.

*   *   *

August 9, 1944

Mission #77

We are still busy busting up transportation with bombs and by strafing. Today we were given the railroad from Metz to Lille—about 150 miles long and were to clean out anything moving. We arrived at Metz on time, I leading blue flight and picked out a very large marshalling yard and bombed it with very good results, starting several fires and destroying tracks and cars.

We then turned northwest and started along the railroad shooting up a few locomotives and other targets. Cargo Squadron found an airdrome and destroyed 10 airplanes on it. Surtax squadron stayed up for top cover, as there were too many planes on the A/D firing and being so crowded we may have had a mid-air collision. After cleaning up the drome we came on home. I was almost hit by heavy flak coming out over Dunkerque.

† L.A. Dicks—killed in action 8/10/44

*   *   *

August 13, 1944 †

Mission #78

This was the most miserable mission I have had thus far due to our taking off at 4:30 in the morning. It was blacker than pitch and was a wonder we didn't kill somebody. We were taking off 4 abreast and one man couldn't get off the ground, ground looped it at the end of the field, tearing up the plane. This same boy was killed in the evening mission today when his controls were shot away over France. He made it back to the field but the last control wire broke as he peeled off for a landing and he went straight in.

After taking off we proceeded toward Orleans which was our area, but it was still very dark and we lost sight of the rest of the Group. I was flying only by instruments all this time and I flew all the way to Orleans on instruments as the sky was still dark.

We circled at Orleans for about 20 minutes reforming our squadron and waiting for it to get light enough to see. The only way we could tell where we were by the reflection in the river. We couldn't even see the city of Orleans even though we were right over it.

We finally bombed the marshalling yards there getting several good hits on the junction and a concentration of cars there. Capt. Conner got two direct hits on a flak car destroying it. We were unable to find anything to shoot up, so we came on home. At least I got back early enough to go to church.

Lt. B.V. Smith—Killed on return from mission
Lt. Fitzgerald—N.Y.R. 8/9/44

*   *   *

August 16, 1944 †

Mission #79

Well, on my 24th Birthday, we had a long escort job, the first in a couple of weeks, too. We were taking 1500 heavies on withdrawal from targets around Leipzig and beyond. We were to take the rear of the formations and help out all stragglers.

We made L/F a little north of Amsterdam and proceed inland across the Zuider Zee to Steinhuder Lake where we turned south east and picked up our bombers. We continued to the end of the Task Force and then started home with them. I was leading Surtax Blue Flight and we picked up a straggler, a Lib and stuck with them to keep off E/A. They kept calling on "C" channel and asking if we would stay with them. After about the third time that we told them we would—they threw out all their guns, ammunition, and every thing that they could to lighten the plane. They were then able to gain a little altitude, as they were too low for comfort. They were afraid they wouldn't make it across the Channel so we stayed with them till they made the English coast. I then pulled up along side and waved good-bye. They were waving like mad and were really happy about us staying with them.

It makes a person feel good to know they are appreciated and those boys really did. I started to land with them to see them, but decided to come on home. No E/A seen but one Group got 16 for a loss of three, which isn't bad.

*   *   *

(while I was at the Flak Home)

Lt. Coss—M.I.A. (Bailed out) 8/26/44
Lt. Col. Gilvert—M.I.A. (crash landed) 8/28/44
Lt. Lacy—M.I.A. 8/28/44

*   *   *

September 1, 1944 † †

Mission #80

This is my first mission since returning from the Flak Home and I felt funny in a plane again. I was Surtax Yellow leader today and our job today was dive bombing and strafing transportation around the area east of Brussels.

We crossed in a little north of Ostende without encountering any flak, in fact my flight didn't receive any flak at all on this mission except some eager English gunner as we came back to England. Just before we reached our area we saw the 56th Group dive bombing and strafing Charleroi Airdrome near Brussels. This is a really "hot" place but they seemed to be doing a good job.

We flew around in our area for about 15 minutes before I picked out a target that looked worth working over. We started our dive at 9,000 feet and pulled out at 3,000 feet, getting several good hits on the marshalling yards, setting some good fires. We then climbed back up to 5,000 feet and began to look for convoys on the roads. Several fights were around cleaning up everything in sight so we went up north a little way and found about 40 trucks stopped under the trees on a road. We went down and all made about 12 passes each and destroyed about 20 trucks loaded with petrol and shot up about 20 others that wouldn't burn. We started out after two of my flight had shot all their ammo and I had fired 1775 rounds leaving 225 rounds. The rest of the Group had already gone home so we came out alone.

On this mission my flight of four put about 40 to 50 trucks out of action in 10 minutes. My claim 8 destroyed and 10 damaged (1—FW-190 destroyed).

Lt. Jones—N.Y.R. 9/1/44
Lt. Dunaway—M.I.A. (bailed out) 9/1/44

*   *   *

September 1, 1944

Mission #81 My Last Mission

This evening our group had another dive bombing and strafing job in the Trier and Luxembourg area. Our squadron wasn't carrying bombs and were to be top cover.

We arrived at Trier about 6:35 and our squadron stayed up high to protect the boys who were dive bombing from enemy fighters. We watched them do a good job of bombing the marshalling yards near Trier then they split up looking for strafing targets. We went down on a convoy of trucks that turned out to be Red Cross vehicles. They were solid on a road for at least five miles—at least 200 of them. Capt. Wolfe shot up one before we identified them, then we left them alone. We were unable to find any other targets so we started on home. We ventured over Namur quite by accident and I almost received a direct hit by flak.

We continued home, coming out the enemy coast between Brugges and Zeebrugges, and on home with nothing further happening.

Major Brown got four 109's on his tail but turned sharply and shot one down, the other three chased him all across Brussels before he got away. Lt. Boettler and his wing man found four ME-110's on the deck and shot them down. This brings the Group's total to 305 planes destroyed.

On returning from this mission I had completed 300 hours and 15 minutes of combat time. Today the tour was shortened to 285 hours, so if I had waited another day I wouldn't have had to fly the last two missions—such is life in the E.T.O

My Last Mission—#81

White Flight

H Capt. Wolfe
M Lt. Hart
C Lt. Stallings
B (aborted—went back)

Felixstowe ----------------- 109° --------------- 5:33
Furnes --------------------- 150° --------------- 5:53
Luxembourg -------------- 137° --------------- 6:30
Lv. Trier Area --------------------------------- 7:15
Furnes --------------------- 301° --------------- 8:12
Felixstone ----------------- 301° --------------- 8:33
Home --------------------- 287° --------------- 8:47

Check Points

(S)—Brussels   (P)—Nancy
(O)—Metz   (H)—Luxembourg

*   *   *

September 12, 1944

Received my orders to report to the Casual Pool, Station 594 Stone, Stafford, Eng. to await shipment to the Zone of Interior (the U.S.A.).

*   *   *

1st Lt. James B. Stallings
133 E. Central Ave.
Moultrie, Georgia

"Lest We Forget"

On the next two pages are the names of the pilots we have lost in the 78th Fighter Group while I was here. Also the dates are listed and what happened to them—to the best of our knowledge.

     M.I.A.—Missing In Action
     N.Y.R.—Not Yet Reported: usually when no one sees or hears what happens to a pilot, and nothing is known except he didn't return.
     K.I.A.—Killed In Action
     P.O.W.—Prisoner Of War
     "*"—Pilots in my squadron
     Evaded—Escaped

     *   *   *

Roll of Honor
(*in the 82nd)

1. Lt. Reese—April 12, 1944—M.I.A. OK
2. *Lt. Roberts—April 13, 1944-M.I.A. (now P.O.W. 7/4/44)
3. Lt. O'Connell—killed April 15, 1944
4. Lt. Ford—83rd Sqdn—M.I.A.
5. *Lt. Steele-believed interned Switzerland (P.O.W.) 5/11/44
6. *Lt. Kosinski—M.I.A. (bailed out) 5/11/44 (evaded)
7. *Lt. Hagarty—M.I.A.(now P.O.W. 7/21/44) 5/12/44
8. *Lt. Hazelett—M.I.A. (bailed out) 5/29/44 K.I.A.
9. *Lt. Orvis—M.I.A. 5/29/44 K.I.A.
10. *Lt. Genge—M.I.A. (bailed out) OK 5/25/44
11. Capt. Juckheim—M.I.A(bailed out)OK 5/29/44 P.O.W. 8/1/44
12. *Capt. Wilkinson—killed on local flight 6/4/44
13. *Lt. Steinwedel—N.Y.R. 6/5/44 K.I.A.
14. Lt. Just—M.I.A. 6/7/44 K.I.A.
15. Lt. Rice—M.I.A. 6/7/44 OK
16. *Lt. Kuehner-6/10/44 K.I.A.
17. *Lt. R.L. Baker—N.Y.R. 6/10/44 K.I.A.
18. Lt. McIntosh-84th Sqdn—M.I.A. 6/10/44 OK

19. Lt. Loyd—84th Sqdn—M.I.A. 6/10/44 K.I.A.
20. Lt. Casey—M.I.A. 6/10/44 OK
21. Lt. Lacey—M.I.A. 6/10/44 OK
22. Capt. Hunt—M.I.A. 6/10/44 K.I.A. 8/10/44
23. Major Stump—M.I.A. 6/10/44 OK
24. Major McLeod—M.I.A. 6/10/44 (evaded to Eng) 8/21/44 OK
25. Lt. McDermott—K.I.A. 6/10/44
26. *Lt. Casey—M.I.A.(bailed out) 6/11/44(evaded) 8/21/44 OK
27. *Capt. Ramsey—K.I.A. 6/13/44
28. *Lt. Hodges—N.Y.R. 6/20/44 K.I.A.
29. Lt. Gibbs—(Tifton,Ga) K.I.A. 6/22/44
30. Lt. Kitley—Killed on T.O. 7/1/44
31. Lt. Riese—Killed on T.O. 7/1/44
32. Lt. Orr—M.I.A. (killed) 7/1/44
33. Lt. Moseley—M.I.A. (bailed out) 7/4/44 OK
34. Lt. Mullins—M.I.A. 7/5/44 K.I.A.
35. Captain Lay—M.I.A.(bailed out) 7/18/44 K.I.A.
36. *Major Munson—K.I.A. 7/19/44
37. Lt. Smith—killed in local crash 7/19/44
38. Lt. Putnam—killed in local crash 7/19/44
39. *Lt. Morris—K.I.A. 7/26/44
40. Lt Korsemeyer—M.I.A. (bailed out) 7/31/44 OK
41. *Capt. Clark—M.I.A. (bailed out) P.O.W. 8/3/44 OK
42. Lt Myler—K.I.A. 8/5/44
43. Lt. Cummings—M.I.A. (bailed out) 8/6/44 OK
44. *Lt. L.A. Dicks—K.I.A. 8/10/44
45. *Lt. B.V. Smith—K.I.A. 8/13/44
46. Capt. Peal—N.Y.R. 8/14/44 K.I.A.
47. *Lt. Fitzgerald—N.Y.R. (P.O.W.) 8/9/44
48. Lt. Miller—K.I.A. 8/18/44
49. *Lt. Coss—M.I.A.(bailed out) 8/26/44
50. Lt.Col.Gilbert—M.I.A(crash landed)8/28/44 evaded 9/10/44
51. Lt. Lacy—M.I.A. 8/28/44 K.I.A.
52. Lt Dunaway—M.I.A. (bailed out) 9/1/44 OK
53. Lt. Jones—N.Y.R. 9/1/44 K.I.A.

*   *   *

Last Known Results

Roberts, D.R.—OK

K.I.A.
Reese, Wm H.
Hazelett, P.H.
Orvis, W.S.
Just, H.H.
Baker, R.L.
Kuehner, R.S.
Loyd, D.T.
Hunt, W.F.
McDermott, W.M.
Ramsey, J.C.
Hodges, B.H.
Kitley, E.T.
Gibbs, O.E. (Rt.4, Tifton, GA)
Orr, R.R.
Mullins, R.E.
Lay, H.T.
Morris, H.J.
Myler, J.J.
Peal, C.M.
Miller, J.B.
Lacy, W.O.
Jones, Y.V.

—The End—

Hunters in the Fog
A Screenplay

Jim Stallings

with

Consultant
James B. Stallings, Sr
(Lt. Col. USAF, Retired)

Screenplay Abbreviations

EXT	Exterior Camera Shot
INT	Interior Camera Shot
INT/EXT	Interior Shot, then Exterior Shot
O.S.	Spoken Off Screen
Cont.	Speech broken but Continued by same speaker

FADE IN:

EXT—AIRFIELD—ENGLAND—EARLY A.M.

INSERT TITLE: U.S. ARMY AIR BASE, OXBRIDGE, ENGLAND, MARCH 1944

The airfield is covered in heavy fog. A ROARING of P-47 Thunderbolt engines can be heard in the distance. Barely visible in the near distance, a road and a fence, pasture, woods. Dimly through the foggy woods, several deer feed.

Suddenly, four abreast, P-47 Thunderbolt fighter plane flights take off, lifting through the fog over the road. There's a muffled GUNSHOT, the deer scatter into the woods, hunters in the fog.

Row after row of fighters take off through the fog. Their wings dip, waver and nearly touch overhead.

INT/EXT—MIKE'S P-47

MIKE CURTIS is a twenty year old U.S. Army Air Corps pilot from Virginia; he has a sharply defined face, bright alert eyes, and a no nonsense, all business glance about flying matters…the face of a gifted pilot, a "natural." But despite the professionalism, there remains in his face the wistfulness of a romantic, a seeker of adventure, although his idealistic innocence is fading fast.

He takes off and glances left and right at the other three P-47s climbing in flight formation after takeoff, just visible in fog. Mike adjusts his position.

INT/EXT—AB'S P-47

CARL "AB" ABERNATHY, twenty-three, a stern, long-faced farm boy from Illinois, is Red Flight Leader. His plane's nickname near cockpit is "Grim Reaper," picture of cowled death sweeping away German fighters with a scythe. On his instrument panel is a good luck charm, a rabbit's foot.

            AB
  Tuck it in, Red Flight.

INT/EXT—JAKE'S P-47

JAKE RUSSELL, twenty, is dark and handsome, and wears an easy, almost cocky smile. He typically appears little worried about his destiny, confident his fate is hooked to a rising star.

                                              JAKE
               Red Four, Roger.

INT/EXT—MIKE'S P-47

Mike looks down at a small photo of a biplane, framed in a small square locket, twirling from the instrument panel.

INT/EXT—PAUL'S P-47

PAUL SALVUCCI, Italian-American from Boston's North End, looks about and smiles. He wears a cross, a Saint's medal hangs over the instrument panel. His plane's nickname painted outside his cockpit is "Hit Man"—a Zoot-suited gangster guns down Nazi planes.

INT—AB'S P-47

Ab stares ahead in a cool, detached, almost dreamy manner.

INT/EXT—MIKE'S P-47

Mike adjusts his position slightly. The squadron breaks out above the fog. Climbing, the squadron hits turbulence. Mike bounces around, steadying the plane.

EXT—SKY—EARLY MORNING

The squadron of fighters climbs toward a sky filled with American bombers, B-17s (Flying Fortresses) & B-24s (Liberators), extending below the horizon to the east.

INT/EXT—MIKE'S P-47

MIKE scans the sky.

                                              MIKE
               Paul, how many in this escort?

INT/EXT—PAUL'S P-47

Paul looks up at bombers.

                                              PAUL
               Sixteen hundred big friends, a max effort!

INT/EXT—JAKE'S P-47

Jake checks his instruments.

                                    JAKE (to Germans)
        Hey out there, if you're listening...can't say
        where it is, but here we come...
        (to Red Flight pilots)
        You know, I visited there with my parents...
        1935, I think. Beautiful old opera house and
        parks, too bad.

INT/EXT—AB'S P-47

Ab looks right and left.

                                    AB
        Red Flight, let's cut the chatter.

EXT—SKY

Fighters assume escort positions along each side of the bombers across Belgium as they head into Germany.

INT/EXT—MIKE'S P-47

Mike glances about, hundreds of aircraft in every direction.

Mike WHISTLES, "Oh Shenandoah." His eyes focus on the small picture of the biplane. The radio CRACKLES.

                                    JAKE O.S.
        Heavy flak, twelve o'clock high!

Ahead flak EXPLODES around the lead flight of bombers.

EXT—SKY

Flak starts EXPLODING with increasing frequency around the bombers and fighters.

INT/EXT—MIKE'S P-47

Nearby flak jolts fighters and bombers. Mike's P-47 bounces from the turbulence and adjusts. Black smoke sweeps past.

BOMPH! Flak explodes between his wing and Paul's plane.

INT/EXT—AB's P-47

Ab looks over at bursts of flak creeping closer.

                                              AB
                        Let's climb out of this flak.

INT/EXT—MIKE'S P-47

Mike as wingman to Element Leader Paul, climbs in unison with Paul, who parallels Flight Leader Ab and his wingman Jake. Flak explodes below them. Mike looks downward.

EXT—SKY BELOW

A bomber is hit with flak. There's an explosion in the wing root, the wing collapses, the bomber spirals downward.

INT/EXT—MIKE'S P-47

Mike looks downward and groans.

                                            MIKE
                        Jesus.

                                            AB O.S.
                        Any chutes?

                                            MIKE
                        Nothing.

INT/EXT—PAUL'S P-47

Paul crosses himself.

                                            PAUL
                        No…

INT/EXT—JAKE'S P-47

Jake shakes his head, chews his lip.

                                            JAKE
                        Tough luck, man oh man.

EXT—SKY

The four planes of Red Flight adjust in relation to other flights of fighters.

Flak explodes throughout the squadrons. A fighter in a distant flight takes spirals down on fire. A chute appears.

INT/EXT—MIKE'S P-47

Mike looks out and down.

           MIKE
  Yeah! He made it out!

           RADIO (group O.S.)
  Made it.

Several flights of American fighters slip in to accompany the bombers. Mike sits up, squints forward.

           AB (O.S.)
  Here's our replacements…

Mike sits up, squints forward.

           MIKE
  Heads up, we've got company. Enemy aircraft,
  dead ahead.

EXT—SKY

German fighter planes (ME-109s) fly toward the lead bombers and begin firing.

EXT—U.S. BOMBERS

All gunners—upper, lower, tail and waist (side)—begin firing back.

EXT—GERMAN FIGHTERS—SKY

The flight of German fighters, firing their guns, swoops through the bombers.

EXT—RED FLIGHT—SKY

Red Flight flies above the bombers.

           AB O.S.
  Let's take 'em down.

Ab's plane drops down left after the flight of German fighters. Jake, Paul and Mike drop off to the follow.

INT/EXT—MIKE'S P-47

Paul's P-47 gives chase after a pair of German fighters.

Mike stays on Paul's tail, providing support.

Paul starts firing. The two German pilots split, one climbing, the other diving.

Paul goes into a climb, Mike in support. Suddenly tracer bullets fly past Mike's cockpit. He looks back.

EXT: SKY ABOVE

An ME-109 German fighter streaks toward Mike.

INT/EXT: MIKE'S P-47

Mike maneuvers to avoid being hit, sticking with Paul.

> MIKE
> Red Three! Red Three! Gotta bogey on my tail, gotta break off!

INT/EXT: PAUL'S P-47

Paul glances back, shakes head.

> PAUL
> Roger, Red Four!

INT/EXT—MIKE'S P-47

Mike dives down and into clouds. Tracers sweep past, THUDS in fuselage from several hits. In thick cloud, Mike does a hard turn and bears down on a complete turnaround. Clouds sweep past, as he watches his instruments.

> MIKE
> Come on, come on.

Mike stares into clouds. As he completes the full circle, he straightens out his turn and accelerates ahead.

Suddenly he's behind the German, both in the open air, below the cloud cover, over the flat farmland of occupied Holland.

EXT—SKY

German fighter drops to tree level. Mike shadows him.

INT/EXT—MIKE'S P-47

Mike fires several bursts into the German fighter. The German fighter starts to smoke.

German fighter drops its landing gear and starts to land at an aerodrome. Mike fires a final burst as it crashes on the runway, exploding.

Ahead are many military aircraft parked on the airfield. Mike fires at them as he passes across the airfield.

EXT—GUN EMPLACEMENTS—AIRFIELD

German soldiers man antiaircraft guns and start firing.

INT/EXT—MIKE'S P-47

Antiaircraft flak is coming up from the field.

EXPLOSIONS sound near him, smoke and percussion shocks. Mike stays on the deck until he is clear of the airfield antiaircraft defense.

Several SHOTS strike his fighter. Mike looks back over his shoulder. There's a pair of German fighters.

          MIKE
  Damn!

Mike goes to full power and climbs into low clouds.

          MIKE (Cont.)
  Balls to the wall!

EXT—CLOUDS

Mike's P-47 breaks through the clouds. Pursued by the two German fighters he skims through the surface of the cloud cover, weaving, avoiding their shots.

INT/EXT—MIKE'S P-47

Mike sweeps into a cloud mass and does a dive and circles back up in the cloud cover coming out behind the Germans. He starts to bear down on them.

          JAKE O.S.
  Hey, need a little help?

Mike looks around, right and left. There's Jake's fighter just above and behind him.

Mike gives him thumbs up. Jake rocks his wings in salute and starts firing.

          MIKE
  They're too far.

INT/EXT—JAKE'S P-47

Jake grins and glances at Mike.

                                          JAKE
    Just saying hello.

He fires off a few more harmless rounds.

EXT—SKY

German fighters accelerate and dive through cloud cover.

                                      JAKE O.S.
    Too thick, we've lost them.

INT/EXT—MIKE'S P-47

Mike looks at his fuel gauge, less than half full.

                                        MIKE
    Red Four, time to head home.

                                      JAKE O.S.
    Red Two, Roger.

INT/EXT—JAKE'S P-47

Jake gives a thumbs up signal.

                                        JAKE
    Bagged a 109, got it on film, confirmed. That's two for me, three to go for ace.

                                      MIKE O.S.
    Congratulations.

                                        JAKE
    You bag your first—

INT/EXT—MIKE'S P-47

Mike is looking down at a B-17, smoke drifting from its engines. Behind it a German fighter shoots at it.

                                        MIKE
    Six o'clock, a Fort in trouble.

EXT—SKY

The two American fighters drop toward the German fighter.

                                      JAKE O.S.
        There's only one, I'll take him and you stick
        with the bomber.

                                      MIKE O.S.
        Roger...

German fighter peels off and Jake's P-47 is in hot pursuit. Mike's P-47 pulls alongside the bomber.

INT/EXT—MIKE'S P-47

Mike looks over at bomber, with the insignia "Lucky Lady", and a Vargas girl pinup. The plane is badly shot up. The fires are contained but still smoking, two engines dead. The crew tosses equipment out the sidedoors. They wave heartily.

                                BOMBER PILOT O.S.
        Little friend! Thank you!

                                       MIKE
        No sweat!

                                BOMBER PILOT O.S.
        That bastard's been on us ever since turnaround...
        got enough fuel to stay with us, give air support?

                                       MIKE
        I'll lead you into the coast.

Mike taps his fuel gauge, under a quarter tank.

INT/EXT—BOMBER

BOMBER PILOT and CO-PILOT are looking out at Mike's plane.

                                BOMBER PILOT
        May have to ditch in the Channel.

                                    MIKE O.S.
        Hey, we'll take the short way home, the emer-
        gency base at Manston.

                              BOMBER CO-PILOT
             Man, I hate that cold water swimming!

EXT—SKY

Mike's P-47 cruises next to the ailing bomber. Jake's P-47 suddenly pulls alongside Mike.

INT/EXT—JAKE'S P-47

Jake looks over at Mike and the bomber. Mike gives a wave.

                                    MIKE O.S.
             Any luck?

                                    JAKE
             No, lost him in the clouds. He headed back into
             Germany. What's this? You got escort duty here?

Jake stares at his low fuel reading.

                                    MIKE O.S.
             Yeah, they're losing altitude.

                                    JAKE
             Well, we get to the Channel, we'll cut for home.
             They're safe then.

INT/EXT—MIKE'S P-47

Mike frowns and looks toward Jake.

                                    MIKE
             I promised I'd stick with them. They may ditch
             in the Channel, they'll need airsea rescue.

                                    JAKE O.S.
             That only takes one fighter. I'll head on in. I'm
             low on fuel.

                                    MIKE
             Suit yourself. I may land at the coast with these
             guys.

                                    JAKE O.S.
             Yeah…maybe, maybe not.

EXT—SKY—LATER

At low altitude the bomber and two fighters reach the Dutch coast and the English Channel appears. The bomber crew continues to throw stuff out.

Jake's P-47 peels off and heads toward the fighter base.

JAKE O.S.
Stay dry now, save you a place at the bar!

BOMBER PILOT O.S.
Hey, you're not leaving us!

MIKE O.S.
Hell no, follow me in.

EXT—SKY

Mike pulls ahead and leads the bomber across the Channel; the cloud cover is low and thick.

INT/EXT—MIKE'S P-47

He taps the fuel gauge and twirls the biplane photo.

MIKE
Come on, come on, you can make it.

BOMBER PILOT O.S.
Gonna be close, Holy Mother.

Mike looks back, the bomber is losing altitude.

MIKE
Give it all you got, we're on target, stick with me.

Bomber's engines rev up slightly, more smoke spewing forth.

EXT—COASTAL AIRBASE

Fire trucks and ambulances are waiting on runway. Rescue crews watch with binoculars. A fireman waves toward the sea.

EXT—RUNWAY & SEA

Mike's P-47 leads the bomber toward the runway. They're skimming over the waves.

INT/EXT—MIKE'S P-47

Mike crosses his fingers.

                    MIKE
    Come on, baby, come on.

INT—BOMBER

The pilot revs the engines for power and lift. The crew lashes down the wounded and crouches down.

EXT—RUNWAY/SEA

Mike's P-47 skims over the beach and over the runway, not touching down.

The bomber skims over the beach, nearly touching the dunes, and skids down the runway.

INT/EXT—MIKE'S P-47

Mike smiles and takes a deep breath. He pulls up and circles the field. Bomber crew (O.S.) CHEERS.

EXT—RUNWAY

The bomber is surrounded by fire trucks and ambulances.

INT/EXT—MIKE'S P-47

Mike banks his plane and stares down at field.

                  BOMBER PILOT O.S.
    You coming down?

                  MIKE
    Nah, I got enough fuel for Oxbridge. Come on
    up for a drink sometime, we've got a great club.

                  BOMBER PILOT O.S.
    Sounds good. My name's TUBBS, JAMES
    TUBBS from Beatrice, Nebraska.

                  MIKE
    Mike Curtis, Culpeper, Virginia.

                  TUBBS O.S.
    We'll be down one day. That's a promise, thanks Curtis.

                                    MIKE
    Look forward to it.

EXT—OXBRIDGE AIRBASE—AFTERNOON

Mike's P-47 lands safely.

EXT—HANGER

Mike's P-47 rolls to a stop.

The GROUND CREW of four men surrounds the plane and climbs up on the wings to the cockpit.

SANDY GEORGE, mid-thirties, is Mike's Crew Chief. He has the battered face of a veteran welter weight fighter. He helps Mike roll back the canopy.

                                    SANDY (to Mike)
    You're running late.

                                    MIKE
    Saw a big friend home.

                                    SANDY
    Looks like we got some repair work.

Mike climbs out and inspects the damage. The crew follows him. Big bullet holes are in the wing and tail section.

                                    SANDY
    You get the bastard back?

                                    MIKE
    Got one of 'em landing.

                                    SANDY
    Way to go, sir!

EXT—OPERATIONS/DEBRIEFING BUILDING

Mike walks up to the building. Ab, Paul, and Jake, still in flight gear, are sitting on the steps. Mike sits down with them and lights a cigarette.

                                    MIKE
    You guys still waiting for debriefing?

JAKE
Hell no! We've had our shot of bourbon...
(points to eggs in a cap)
and we've earned our farm fresh for breakfast tomorrow.

PAUL
We were just shootin' the bull and...waiting for you.

AB
You get those guys home okay?

MIKE
Lucky Lady, yeah, she made it...man, what a mission!

JAKE
Say, Mike, remember in training when you told me how bored you were back home Virginny, how you wanted some action?

MIKE
Yeah...maybe. You wish you were back at Yale snoozing and boozing?

JAKE
Yeah, yeah...can you see him, guys, flying that circus plane, a regular Walter Mitty smalltown ace.

PAUL (to Jake)
Hey, Mike beat you out in cadet training, didn't he, Jake?

JAKE
Yo paisan, I didn't waste my high school years gophering around some hick airfield!

PAUL (to Mike/Jake)
Just the same, we gotta survive three hundred combat hours to finish a tour of duty, and Ab and I are halfway done. You two are still shy your first hundred.

JAKE
Big deal…

                    AB
Before my first mission, the Intelligence Chief
told us, he says, the first hundred hours you're just
learning to be a fighter pilot, then that second
hundred hours, maybe you're of some use to us
finally, but that last hundred hours, he says, you
start thinking, hey, I might just survive, and then,
boys, you're hardly worth a damn, you're just playing it safe, trying to get home alive, back to the ZI.

                    PAUL (to Mike/Jake)
The ZI, Zone of the Interior, Stateside baby.
Dreamland…

Jake shakes his head derisively, smiles broadly, confidently. Behind him in doorway
FIRST LIEUTENANT JERRY WATSON, a twenty-four year old Intelligence
Officer, wearing wire-rimmed glasses, studies a clipboard.

                    WATSON (to group)
Okay, you're all done but Curtis, we need a few
words with you.

INT—DEBRIEFING ROOM

Maps cover the walls. Mike sits facing Lieutenant Watson and CAPTAIN HARRY
"DOC" LEWIS, mid-thirties, the Flight Surgeon. He has a casual, slightly rum-
pled look. On the desk is a bottle of whiskey, a shot glass and two eggs.

                    WATSON
Like I said, at the moment we got two pilots
M.I.A, Jenkins and Steinmetz. Jenkins' plane
disintegrated, but Steinmetz hit his chute…
Congratulations on the kill, Curtis. You got
anything else, Doc?

                    DOC
You gonna want a shot of bourbon, Lieutenant?

                    MIKE
No sir.

Doc picks up the shot glass and the bottle with the remaining bourbon. He checks a small notebook.

> DOC
> You're approaching one hundred combat hours, aren't you?

> MIKE
> Ninety-six hours as of today.

> DOC
> Ready for a rest?

> MIKE
> Nope.

Doc looks him over and smiles.

> DOC
> Just wait 'til you've hit two hundred hours, I won't have to ask.

Mike smiles confidently.

> MIKE
> Two hundred hours, the sooner the better.

Doc nods in agreement. They stand and Mike picks up his two eggs and leaves the debriefing room.

EXT—ROAD—DAY

Mike crosses a road that divides the base, leaving operations, hangers and runways behind him. He enters through a gate into the other half of the base holding the barracks, administrative offices, parade grounds, dining halls, officer and enlisted men's clubs.

EXT—NEAR BARRACKS—DAY

Mike walks along. Hears a CAR HORN and turns. Paul waves Mike over to a Land Rover parked behind the dining hall.

Paul stands with a group of two men and two women in hunting clothes. The rear of the car is open and two dead deer lay there on the tailgate.

EDITH COWAN, about twenty years old, a red-haired, attractive woman stands next to Paul.

THOMAS STANFORD, late sixties, is a distinguished English aristocrat, great-uncle to MARGRET TOLAND, who stands next to him. Margret is about twenty and has a strikingly open, noble face. Mike can't take his eyes off her at first glance; he's never seen anyone quite like her. ROBERT BERKSRUN, early twenties, is rather aristocratic, a friendly smile, intellectual-looking.

>PAUL (to Mike)
>Hey, we've got visitors.

>MIKE
>Yes, well, hello.

>OTHERS
>Hello.

Mike's eyes linger on Margret's beautiful face.

>PAUL (to Mike)
>This is Edith Cowan, the lady I been telling you about.

Mike blinks, smiles at Margret, who smiles slightly, and Mike turns his attention to Edith.

>MIKE (to Edith)
>Oh yes, your friend at Cambridge University, how do you do? Mike Curtis.

>EDITH
>Hello, this is Margret Toland and her great uncle Thomas Stanford and Margret's friend, Mr. Robert—

>ROBERT
>That's Berksrun. How do you do?

Mike shakes hands with the three.

>PAUL
>They're donating deer for our mess.

                                    MIKE
         That's awfully nice.

                                    STANFORD
         Least we could do for you chaps. My lands
         adjoin the field.

                                    PAUL (to Mike)
         Here, give me a hand, I was just accepting the
         contribution for the Army Air Corps.

                                    MIKE
         You bet, thanks.

Mike hesitates, holding the eggs, and Margret extends her hands. He hands them to her.

                                    MIKE
         Tomorrow's breakfast.

                                    MARGRET
         Oh, fresh eggs, how wonderful.

Mike and Paul pick up a deer and start to haul it inside. Stanford and Berksrun take the other deer and follow.

But a crew of cooks appear and hurry down the stairs to take the deer in hand.

Mike borrows a rag from one of the cooks and wipes off blood on his hand from the deer.

                                    HEAD COOK
         We'll get that, sir, and many thanks, we'll being
         serving a venison meal tomorrow evening
         then.

HEAD COOK nods at Paul and Mike, prompting them.

                                    PAUL
         Oh.

                                    MIKE
         We insist you join us, please.

                                    STANFORD
         Well, why not?

OTHERS

Yes.

MIKE

It's a date then, (to Headcook) six?

HEADCOOK

Six as usual.

STANFORD

Splendid.

They turn to go, but Margret suddenly remembers the eggs.

MARGRET

Oh, here, I'm sorry.

MIKE

Keep them.

MARGRET

No, I couldn't.

MIKE

Come on, humor me.

MARGRET

Very well, Mike, thanks.

MIKE

Goodbye, 'til tomorrow.

The English group climbs in the car and drives away.

PAUL (to Mike)

Come on, Jenkins is M.I.A., but it's clear he bought it, crashed nose-in strafing an airfield.

Mike shakes his head sadly, then follows Paul.

INT—DINING ROOM—OFFICER'S CLUB

The officers have assembled in the slightly darkened room. They stand in a circle holding lighted candles.

Paul and Mike slip through the door and light candles from the others' candles. Jake and Ab nod from nearby.

COLONEL DODGE, mid-thirties, ace pilot and Commanding Officer, CLEARS HIS THROAT.

                      DODGE
        Ed Jenkins came over with me in '43. In those days they met us at the Channel. It's tough now, it was brutal then, fifty percent loss rate. This was his second tour. He was a fine pilot and a great, quiet man, no one better to fight and die with. We're gonna miss you, Ed.

                      GROUP
        Here! Here!

An officer points to a step ladder. They clear a path and the Colonel climbs the ladder. Under the heavy wooden beams he blackens in the name: "Major Ed Jenkins, 3-28-44." He leaves the candle burning on top of the ladder illumining the name. Many other names line the beams.

He climbs down. They all douse their candles. The name of Ed Jenkins glows above them.

                      DODGE
        Group, atten—shun!

They stand at attention and salute, silence for a moment.

                      DODGE (Cont.)
        Dismissed.

Mike and Paul, Jake and Ab leave together. Dodge remains, lighting up a cigarette, studying the names on the spars.

EXT—PARADE GROUND/BARRACKS—DAY

Mike, Paul, Jake and Ab walk across the parade ground toward the barracks. A Collie dog trots out to meet them.

                      MIKE
        That's Jenkins' dog, SHEP. Who's gonna take care of him?

Mike pets the dog.

                              JAKE
He's bad luck now, right Ab?

                              AB
Maybe... Jenkin's roommate, DOUGLAS, he'll take him.

                              MIKE
Oh come on, this dog's not responsible for Jenkins' bad luck.

Mike pets the dog. The others don't touch the dog.

                              AB
Listen!

The other three stop and listen. There's a distant BUZZING.

                              PAUL
V-1 rocket.

                              AB
Come on.

Ab starts jogging. The others follow. The dog runs after them. They stop under the entrance to the barracks.

                              PAUL
It's passing over, Ab!

                              AB
You never know.

The sound dissipates, silence, DISTANT EXPLOSION. The dog runs off across the field.

                              JAKE
See, bad luck.

Mike laughs. Ab and Paul don't.

INT—PILOTS' ROOM—AFTERNOON

Plain barracks with pinup girls on the walls, photos of airplanes on the door, simple shelves stacked with personal effects anchored to walls, and uniforms hanging under the shelves. A RADIO plays Glenn Miller. Jake, Mike, Ab and Paul are reading their censored mail from home.

JAKE
Whoa! Dad's got no opposition in the primary for his House seat. It's a cakewalk for the fall! Maybe we can bounce Roosevelt.

PAUL
Yeah, dream on…say, you figure your dad will give up that seat for you one day? I dunno 'bout you Republicans, you kinda like that power… you may have to knock off the old man.

JAKE
Republicans take care of their own, I don't see the Democratic Irish doing a helluva lot for the Italians in Boston.

PAUL
Well, we take care of our own, too, in our own way, it's all the same.
(to everyone)
My mother says she fixed my favorite food, calamari, on my birthday and set a place for me.

AB
What's calamari?

PAUL
That's squid to you barbarians.

Mike, Ab, and Jake make faces. Paul reads silently.

PAUL (Cont.)
My Aunt Julianna still wants me to be a priest…

JAKE
Edith know that yet? What the hell will you do?

PAUL
I don't know…I've been thinking about going to college, maybe teaching high school math.

                              AB

You're damned good with numbers and naviga-
tion charts.

                              JAKE

Don't try out for English teacher!

                              PAUL

Very funny…
(reads more)
Gee, and they sang happy birthday to me…

Ab, absently, gazes at Paul.

                              AB

That's nice, that's nice.

                              MIKE

Ab, what's up in Illinois?

                              AB

My dad's about the same, the stroke keeps him
bedridden. My younger brother's doing the
spring plowing, he's fifteen. They could use me
right now…

                              PAUL

Hey, you're brother will do fine…like I always
tell you, it's in your blood, all that corn. I went
out there once, man, corn, I almost panicked,
it's everywhere, like the ocean!

                              AB

Yeah, corn'll do that sometimes, specially later
in the summer.

                              JAKE

What the hell, Ab, you'll be home before the
corn's knee high.

Ab looks at them one by one as if memorizing their faces.

                              AB

I'd like that better than anything.

                                        JAKE
              So what's with your dad's drugstore, Mike?
              People building a shrine to their winged hero
              out of malt cups?

                                        MIKE
              Yeah, right…my sister says there was a tornado
              hit near the airport and damaged the hangar.
              My Stearman's okay…

                                        PAUL
              What do you call it?

Jake's smoking and blows out a jet of smoke.

                                        JAKE
              An airplane!

Ab laughs.

                                        JAKE (points at Ab)
              Now there's a man with a genuine sense of
              humor.

                                        MIKE (to Paul)
              Shenandoah.

                                        JAKE
              Hey, I'm gettin' choked up here, you don't
              need a sissy name like that in the E.T.O.

                                        PAUL (to Jake)
              What's with you today?

Jake jumps up and leaves the room and enters hallway.

                                        JAKE O.S.
              COLSON! You confirm that kill?

                                        PAUL
              What a hotshot!

                                        JAKE O.S.
              When do we do the name thing!?

Colson SHOUTS something back unintelligible.

                             PAUL
         He'll buck his way to Squadron Commander,
         wanta bet?

Jake pops back in the room.

                             JAKE
         Come on, you deadbeats, showtime.

EXT—HANGER—OXBRIDGE AIR BASE—LATE AFTERNOON

Mike, Jake, Ab and Paul, LT. COLSON, the CREW CHIEFS, other PILOTS, and PHOTOGRAPHERS have gathered around two P-47s.

                             COLSON
         Okay, who do we start with?

                             JAKE
         Ladies first, Mike.

                             COLSON
         Lieutenant Curtis, step this way.

The group is gathered in front of Mike's P-47. A cloth curtains the area just in front of the cockpit.

Mike steps forward. Mike's crew chief, Sandy George, and other ground crew climb up the wing to curtain.

                             COLSON
         With the general approval of your mates, your
         P-47 number four-seven-two-zero-eight is hereby
         renamed—

OFFICER motions and groundman drops curtain. His insignia reads, "EAGLE EYE," an eagle, wings spread, talons outstretched, diving after Nazi fighter planes.

APPLAUSE. Cameras start flashing. Mike is delighted.

                             MIKE
         Thanks, guys, great job.

                             SANDY
         It was Jessup, sir,

                              JESSUP
              I just did the finishing work.

                              MIKE
              Beautiful job, thanks.

                              JAKE (to Mike)
              Eagle Eye, who woulda guessed?

                              MIKE
              Come on, let's see your tattoo.

They troop over to Jake's plane.

                              COLSON
              Lieutenant Russell, step forward.

Jake steps forward and smiles proudly.

                              COLSON (Cont.)
              With the approval of your squadron, your P-47
              number seven-six-four-four-three is hereby
              renamed—

The curtain drops. The insignia reads "BOUNTY HUNTER"—a smoking six gun blows a Nazi plane out of the sky. APPLAUSE.

                              JAKE
              Looks good, looks good,
              (to photographer)
              Get a close up, will you? I want this in the
              papers back home.

                              COLSON
              You'll get a press release back home, both of you.

                              JAKE
              Eagle Eye over there, he doesn't care, do you?

Mike shrugs and smiles. Ab and Paul look on. The flash bulbs pop. Rain sprinkles down.

                              JAKE (Cont.)
              Now the four of us, come on, it's starting to
              rain…after this the officer's bar…we've got a
              bon voyage party.

Mike, Ab, Paul and Jake pose in front of "BOUNTY HUNTER." The photographer's camera flashes. The rain pours down, the pilots run for cover in the hangar.

INT—OFFICER'S BAR—NIGHT

Jake, Mike, Ab, and Paul join other pilots in toasting two departing pilots. They raise their beer mugs and salute them, and SING "For he's a jolly good fellow."

EXT—OXBRIDGE HANGAR AREA—EARLY MORNING

Rain. Parked rows of P-47s, just visible in the mist.

INT—BRIEFING ROOM—EARLY MORNING

The pilots sit in chairs while being briefed for the mission. Colonel Dodge stands before huge wall map and chalk board filled with take-off times, compass headings. Lt. Watson, other intelligence officers, and Flight Surgeon Doc Lewis observe from the sidelines. Outside, heavy rain.

>   DODGE
> The weather report isn't good, I'm waiting for
> an update.

Ab's holding a cup of coffee in his right hand, which starts to shake slightly; he puts both hands around the cup to steady it. Paul notices but keeps focused on Dodge. Doc Lewis also notices from the sidelines.

>   DODGE (Cont.)
> Call sign for today is Coach.

An officer enters a side door and delivers a note to Dodge who immediately reads it.

>   DODGE (Cont.)
> We'll launch early and try to beat the soup.
> Let's hit it...

There's an audible groan as the pilots start filing out.

>   PAUL
> Hey, cheer up you guys, we're having venison
> for dinner...

The other, more pessimistic, pilots look at him skeptically.

EXT—RUNWAY—MORNING

Red Flight, four abreast, takes off, just visible in rain.

INT/EXT—MIKE'S P-47—MORNING

Mike looks out through the clouds and rain, and can barely see the other three planes in Red Flight.

> AB O.S.
> We're nearing the Channel. Man, this is pea soup! Please God, cancel this one!

The radio CRACKLES with static.

> CONTROLLER O.S.
> Coach, calling Coach, this is Manston Control, return, we repeat, return to base.

> MIKE
> All right, Ab, you and God are pretty tight!

Red Flight begins its turnaround.

EXT—OFFICERS CLUB—NIGHT

Raining, foggy.

INT—OFFICERS CLUB DINING HALL

The officers are finishing the venison steak dinner. Mike sits at the head table with the honored guests, Thomas Stanford, Edith Cowan, Margret Toland, and Robert Berksrun, Colonel Dodge, Paul, Ab and Jake, and other officers.

> MIKE (to Margret)
> Did you shoot these deer?

> MARGRET
> Well one, Uncle got the other. Do you hunt, Lieutenant?

> MIKE
> I've done a lot of deer hunting in Virginia, yes.

Stanford, chatting with Colonel Dodge, smiles at his niece.

> PAUL
> Watch out, Mike, she's a good shot.

> MIKE
> We could use her in the squadron.

JAKE

Yeah, she could use your plane.

Margret frowns, looks down.

EDITH

Margret lost a brother in the RAF.

MIKE

I'm sorry to hear that.

MARGRET

He died in the early days of the blitz, and my father and another uncle were permanently disabled after the First World War, gasings, I'm not much on war anymore.

MIKE

But what can we do?

MARGRET

Go on, I guess, but it seems such a waste.

MIKE

We've got to stop Hitler and the rest… Mussolini and Hirohito.

MARGRET

Of course we do, but you Yanks need to understand our history over here. Germany dominates the center of Europe, it's the locomotive that drives the whole business…so regardless of who's in power, Germany must be dealt with. Hitler will pass, Germany's role in history will not. Too many leaders only see the short term!

EDITH

Don't get Margret started.

ROBERT

No, don't get her started.

MIKE (to Robert)

What are you studying?

> ROBERT
> I'm back and forth now, between statistical studies at Cambridge and War Department research on bombing stats down in London. We're developing more sophisticated statistical models with your Mission Planning in London.

> PAUL
> Oh, what sort of sampling models are you using?

Robert looks uncomfortable and looks at Margret and Edith, there's an awkward pause.

> JAKE
> Paul's our resident mathematician.

> ROBERT (to Paul)
> Sorry, old chum, afraid I'm not at liberty to say.

> PAUL
> That's okay, I understand.

> MARGRET
> He's living on the trolleys, back and forth all the time.

Robert laughs and lights a cigarette.

> ROBERT
> Yes, I don't know which way I'm going anymore.

> MIKE (to Margret)
> Let me guess, you're studying celestial mechanics?

> MARGRET
> No, thank god! Philosophy, history, literature, that sort of thing.

> MIKE
> That sounds interesting. What will you do, teach or something?

> MARGRET
> Something is more like it, but I'd like to write, travel.

MIKE
After the war, you'll have a chance.

JAKE
You can visit America and sample small town life with Mike here. He can give you a ride in his biplane.

MARGRET
I'd like that.

JAKE
Then you can come up to New York and I'll show you the town.

MARGRET
I saw New York when I was fourteen, but I suppose there's more to offer a young woman in her twenties.

JAKE
You bet, especially a single woman.

Margret picks up a cigarette. Jake reaches forward and lights Margret's cigarette, beating Robert's effort.

Talk stops. The SHRILL ENGINE of a V-1 rocket overhead.

EDITH
I just hate those things!

STANFORD
Oh, compared to trench warfare in France they're nothing, more like mosquitoes, something to swat.

DODGE
Unless you're on the receiving end of its bite!

The sound dissipates and no explosion is heard. The conversations in the hall pick up again. Robert glances at his watch and Margret.

MARGRET
Uncle, I need to be going.

                                          EDITH
Oh, we were going to play the slots here at the club.

                                           PAUL
Yeah, we wanted to fleece you high rollers.

                                         STANFORD
No chance there, young man, the war's done that.

                                         MARGRET
Edith, please stay, I've got those essays to prepare.

                                          EDITH
Oh, you're right,
(to Paul)
she's a better scholar, without her I'd have bailed out long ago.

                                           PAUL
Always wear your chute.

                                         MARGRET
That's good advice for us all.

Everyone laughs and gets up.

EXT—PARKING LOT—DINING HALL—NIGHT

Raining, clearing up somewhat. The English party climbs in their car. Mike helps Margret in.

                                           MIKE
I'd like to see you again.

Margret looks surprised.

                                         MARGRET
Come to Cambridge with Paul when he sees Edith, your next day off.

                                           MIKE
I never know when that is, may be two, three days.

                                                MARGRET
    Surprise me then, goodnight.

                                                MIKE
    Goodnight.

Margret waves goodbye. Jake stands nearby.

                                                JAKE (to Mike)
    Hey, give it up, she's a blue blood! You're outgunned!

                                                MIKE
    I'll take my chances.

                                                PAUL
    That a boy!

                                                JAKE
    Don't say I didn't warn you.

                                                MIKE (to Jake)
    Who needs Nazis with friends like you!

Jake laughs and flashes him the victory sign.

EXT—RUNWAY—OXBRIDGE AB—DAWN

Stormy. Squadrons line up for take-off, four abreast.

EXT—MIKE'S PLANE

Eagle Eye symbol and cockpit lashed by wind and rain.

INT/EXT—MIKE'S P-47

Mike looks out at 500 pound bombs under wings.

                                                JAKE O.S.
    Hey, what's the holdup?

                                                MIKE
    This wind, we're overloaded.

                                                PAUL O.S.
    Yeah, no crowding.

                                                AB O.S.
    Listen up, there goes Blue Flight.

EXT—RUNWAY

Blue Flight ahead of Red Flight takes off.

INT/EXT—BLUE FLIGHT P-47

Plane in fog and mist. Pilot LIEUTENANT DOUGLAS panics, surrounded by cloud cover, loses his orientation.

                                DOUGLAS
         I'm losing power!

Douglas almost hits another P-47, stalls out, loses it.

EXT—MEADOW

Douglas' P-47 crashes and EXPLODES.

EXT—RUNWAY

Red Flight sits ready for takeoff.

INT/EXT—MIKE's P-47

Mike stares ahead at the distant, exploding fire.

                              AIR CONTROLLER O.S.
     Cleared for take-off, Red Flight.

                              JAKE O.S.
        Somebody buy it?

                              AB O.S.
        Stick to business!

The planes roll forward for take-off.

EXT—RUNWAY

Red Flight accelerates down runway, weighed down by bombs.

INT—AB'S P-47

Ab is sweating, his eyes bulging.

INT—JAKE'S P-47

Jake stares ahead expectantly.

INT—PAUL's P-47

Paul crosses himself and increases power for liftoff.

INT—MIKE's P-47

Near runway's end, Mike throttles to full power for liftoff.

EXT—RUNWAY END

Red Flight just clears revetments at the runway's end.

INT/EXT—MIKE'S P-47

Climbing through a break in mist, Mike looks down at the burning plane.

INT/EXT—AB's P-47

Ab stares ahead, doesn't look down.

> JAKE O.S.
> Douglas, that poor bastard, Jesus.

A bird or something strikes Ab's cockpit.

> AB
> What the hell?! You see that?

> JAKE O.S.
> Didn't see anything. You know what I'm thinking, Ab?

> AB
> What?

INT/EXT—JAKE'S P-47

Jake looks over at Ab.

> JAKE
> Douglas, he's been feeding that collie, Jenkins' dog. He's a damned dog of death, you ask me.

INT/EXT—PAUL'S P-47

Paul glares in Jake's direction.

> PAUL
> Can it, Russell!

INT/EXT—MIKE'S P-47

Mike shakes his head in dismay.

        MIKE
   Gotta Channel radio check.

INT/EXT—JAKE'S P-47

Jake adjusts his radio.

        JAKE
   Roger, how we doing Ab?

INT—AB'S P-47

Ab is coming unglued. He suddenly hears a PINGING sound. He checks instrument panel, taps gauges, his hand shakes.

EXT—RADIO SHACK—ENGLISH COAST

Rain sweeps over radio shack overlooking English Channel.

INT—RADIO SHACK

RADAR OPERATOR watches screen and sends out coded messages.

INT/EXT—MIKE'S P-47

Radio squeals with static. Mike makes coded notations.

        MIKE
   Okay, we're all set.

INT/EXT—AB'S P-47

Ab swallows repeatedly, sweat on his face.

        MIKE O.S.
   We're clear, Ab.

        AB
   I got problems.

INT/EXT—PAUL'S P-47

Paul looks toward Ab's plane.

                                                    PAUL
    What's up, Red Leader?

INT/EXT—AB'S P-47

Ab runs his hand over his sweating face.

                                                    AB
    I'm sick, I'm breathing fumes, going on hundred
    percent oxygen.

INT/EXT—JAKE'S P-47

Jake shakes his head derisively.

                                                    JAKE
    Come on, Ab, you can shake it off.

                                                    AB O.S.
    I don't think so.

INT/EXT—PAUL'S P-47

Paul checks his watch.

                                                    PAUL
    Ab, it's your call.

INT/EXT—AB'S P-47

Ab can barely hold the stick.

                                                    AB
    I'm turning back, I'm sorry, guys.

INT/EXT—MIKE's P-47

Mike looks out his cockpit and watches Ab peeling off, heading back to base. Jake, as wingman, follows him back.

                                                    MIKE
    We can handle it, Ab.

                                                    AB O.S.
    I know you can.

INT/EXT—JAKE'S P-47

Jake shakes his head.

                         JAKE
    See you guys at the bar.

EXT—RUNWAY—OXBRIDGE

Ab and Jake land and taxi to hangar.

EXT—AB'S P-47—HANGAR

CREW CHIEF and CREW surround Ab's plane. Ab has slumped forward in cockpit. Crew can't get cockpit open.

A jeep pulls up with Doc Lewis and Colonel Dodge.

                    CREW CHIEF
    Ab, open up, the brass is here.

Doc appears next to cockpit.

                       DOC
    Step back, fellas, don't rush him.

INT/EXT—AB'S P-47

Ab stares straight ahead, rain running down the cockpit glass, faces of the crew just beyond.

EXT—BARRACKS—AFTERNOON

Mike and Paul, still in combat suits, walk toward barracks. Jake steps exits the barracks.

                  MIKE (to Jake)
    How's Ab?

                     JAKE
    Ahhh, he's okay, he got channel fever from seeing Douglas nose in.

                     PAUL
    They went through training together, you know, good buddies.

                    MIKE
Yeah, and he's always had that premonition he's not going to make it...like a black cloud over him.

                    PAUL
Well, he dreamed he saw his name on the rafters...what would you think?

                    JAKE
Hell, it's that bad luck attitude he brought from Illinois...

Shep, the collie, runs up to them.

                    JAKE (to Shep)
Beat it!

Shep runs back a few steps in fear.

                    PAUL
Hey!

                    MIKE
He didn't do a damn thing to you.

                    JAKE
Oh yeah.

Jake kicks at the dog. Mike grabs Jake, they tussle briefly, until Paul separates them. Nearby other OFFICERS watch.

                    PAUL
Knock it off!

                    JAKE
Get rid of the jinx, Curtis, or I will, one between the eyes. Jenkins, Douglas, who's next?

                    MIKE
You don't understand...I had a dog like this when I was a kid...

                    PAUL
What happened to him?

MIKE
A car got him...

JAKE
Yeah, so?

MIKE
So, I'll take care of this guy.

JAKE
Not in my barracks, you won't.

PAUL
It's not a good idea.

MIKE
Then I'm taking him over to the MPs 'til I can find a home for him.

JAKE (to Mike)
Bleedin' heart, he'll get you killed.

MIKE
I already killed him...

JAKE
What?!

MIKE
I was drunk...right after I got my driving license...stupidest thing, backed right over him...

Jake throws up his hands.

JAKE
Is everybody goin' nuts? Hey, I'm sorry, but bad luck happens...just do me a favor, Mike, keep him away from me!

Jake marches off toward the Officer's Club.

JAKE (Cont.)
Jesus, now I really need a drink!

PAUL (to Mike)
Hey, he didn't mean anything.

                              MIKE

     The guy gets to me.

                              PAUL

     Jesus, don't let him know that.

                              MIKE

     Come 'ere, Shep.

Mike rubs the dog's head.

                              MIKE (Cont.)
     I'm taking him over, see you later at the memorial
     for Douglas.

Paul watches Mike walk off, playing with Shep.

                              MIKE (to Shep)
     Good boy, we'll find you a home.

EXT—CAMBRIDGE—DAYS

Cambridge, England. A staff car drives into Cambridge.

EXT—STREET—CAMBRIDGE UNIVERSITY—DAY

Mike gets out of staff car, and watches it drive off. He crosses the narrow street and enters a gate to the college.

EXT—COURTYARD—DAY

Mike walks across a courtyard and enters a library.

INT—LIBRARY

Mike finds Margret at a reading table buried in books. Mike picks one up and looks at title.

                              MIKE
     German philosophy, in German…

Margret looks at her watch in surprise.

                              MARGRET
     Oh dear.

                              MIKE
     Am I early?

                          MARGRET
            Oh no, just prompt…come on, we'll take a walk…

Margret throws on a sweater and walks out with Mike.

EXT—COURTYARD—DAY

They pass through an arch, enter courtyard, and walk around the medieval university grounds.

                          MIKE
            You wouldn't know there's a war inside the
            University, so peaceful.

                          MARGRET
            Yes, I came up here to get away from the blitz
            and to study.

                          MIKE
            German literature?

                          MARGRET
            Truth is, I adore philosophy, especially German
            philosophy.

                          MIKE
            Oh my god, Nazism!

                          MARGRET
            No, nineteenth century philosophy. It's far
            more complex than practical British thinking.
            You know, truth is, the Germans are the most
            educated people worldwide.

                          MIKE
            Well, maybe, but the Nazis? They're hardly
            advanced…they're bullies.

                          MARGRET
            We must finally accommodate them through
            negotiation.

MIKE

Sounds like Chamberlain and the America First crowd. Believe me, the Allies aren't stopping at the Channel, we're going to Berlin.

MARGRET

You never know what politicians will do. I've heard rumblings from my pacifist diplomatic friends in London. Come on, enough of politics and philosophy, time for a beer.

Mike gives a thumbs up, and she takes his arm and escorts him out a college gate onto the streets.

EXT—PUB—STREET—DAY

Margret and Mike enter the RED LION PUB.

INT—RED LION

Paul and Edith, Jake and LAUREN STEVENS are present. Lauren is a young British woman in her twenties, wearing a U.S.O. uniform. They're drinking beer. Mike and Margret approach.

JAKE

You know Lauren Stevens?

MARGRET

How do you do.

MIKE

Oh yes, hello again, you organized the last dance function.

LAUREN

Now we've got a big show planned, Bob Hope and Francis Langford.

JAKE

There's talk Bing may come along.

MARGRET

Bing?

JAKE
Don't play high brow, Bing Crosby.

MARGRET
Oh, the singer.

JAKE
Now you're cooking. You should get out of the books.

MIKE
She's been hunting, hasn't she? Remember the venison steaks?

JAKE
Hunting's too solitary.

EDITH
Oh, leave her alone, Jake.

MARGRET
I don't mind, he's cute.

MIKE
Cute?

JAKE
A man who just bagged his third Nazi…two away fron ace. No, aggravating maybe, but not cute. That's demeaning.

MARGRET
My apologies, Ace.

JAKE (to Mike)
You better watch this one, she's like one of those bluebloods at your Southern finishing schools. Can't you hear that Southern Belle in that British accent?

MIKE
Hmmm, Miss Scarlet?

JAKE
Exactly, Vivian Leigh, she was British anyway.

Mike peers at Margret who primps and speaks like Scarlett.

MARGRET (to Mike)
Frankly, Rhett, do you give a damn?

MIKE
Scarlett, why of course I do.

The group laughs at the accuracy of the staged accents.

JAKE (to Mike)
Well, ask her to the dance?

MIKE
Oh.

JAKE
If you don't, I will.

LAUREN (to Jake)
Hey! You're my escort, remember? You're handling the VIP awards.

JAKE
Oh yeah, just kidding.

LAUREN
What a prince!

MIKE (to Margret)
Want to?

MARGRET
Yes?

MIKE
Attend the dance?

MARGRET
I'm not a great dancer.

PAUL
You'll get lots of practice, we learn together.

MARGRET
Oh, a circle dance.

                    EDITH
Wear comfortable pumps.

                    JAKE
Yeah, Mike'll wear his combat boots, be prepared. You know, he's secretly in the infantry.

The group laughs good-naturedly.

                    JAKE (to Mike)
Hey, Steinmetz was officially listed as a POW today.

                    Mike
At least he's alive.

                    JAKE
And did you hear about Ab?

                    MIKE
No.

                    JAKE
Flak home, down on the coast.

                    MIKE
That's good.

                    MARGRET
Flak home?

                    PAUL
Rest for fatigued pilots.

                    MARGRET
It must be very stressful. I saw that crash the other day.

                    JAKE
You saw that happen?

                    MARGRET
No, my Uncle and I were driving by later. What a horrible mess.

JAKE
We were overloaded, carrying five hundred pound bombs, and now we're trying out rockets. It's something new all the time.

PAUL
Flying guinea pigs, that's us.

MIKE
Hey, let's cut the shop talk.

LAUREN
That's what we do in the U.S.O., listen to lots of shop talk.

Edith kisses Paul on the cheek.

EDITH
I'm a good listener, aren't I?

Paul kisses her on the ear.

PAUL
You've got great scoops.

From across the room, a MILITARY DRIVER approaches.

DRIVER (to Paul)
Lieutenant, the car is here.

PAUL
We'll be right there, gotta go.

The three men make quick farewells and head for the door. Suddenly, Mike SNAPS his fingers. He runs back to the table to Margret. Margret smiles at Mike.

MARGRET
Yes?

MIKE
Want an orphaned Collie dog? A fine fellow and companion.

Margret and the other women laugh.

MARGRET
Well, hmmm, I don't mind, but he'd have to stay at my uncle's estate where he can roam.

MIKE
Sounds good.

MARGRET
I'll come around tomorrow.

MIKE
About five?

MARGRET
Yes, I can do that.

MIKE
Terrific, at the Officer's Club.

Margret answers in Southern accent, Mike returning it.

MARGRET
Goodbye, Lieutenant.

MIKE
Good evening, mam, and ladies.

Tips his hat and withdraws.

INT/EXT—COL. DODGE'S P-47—SUNNY SKY OVER HOLLAND

Four planes of Red Flight fly toward English Channel.

Ab, as Flight Leader, has been replaced by Colonel Dodge.

DODGE
There's been reports of troop movements in Holland, so keep an eye peeled for—

JAKE O.S.
Targets of opportunity, yes sir.

DODGE
Correct, Lieutenant. See anything, give a yell.

INT/EXT—JAKE'S P-47

Jake, the Colonel's wingman, looks down.

EXT—DUTCH LANDSCAPE

Aerial view of roads and bridges.

> JAKE O.S.
> Looks pretty innocent.

INT/EXT— PAUL'S P-47

Paul studies the ground, shakes his head.

> PAUL
> Clear from here, farmers, spring plowing, canal boats, standard tourist stuff, sir.

INT/EXT—MIKE'S P-47

Mike peers down at the countryside.

> DODGE O.S.
> Well, let's head for home. Lieutenant Curtis, anything?

EXT—DUTCH LANDSCAPE

A narrow, straight road, poplar trees and their shadow circles, freshly turned fields to the side.

INT/EXT—MIKE'S P-47

Mike looks back into the cockpit and is about to speak. He does a double-take out the left side and squints.

> DODGE O.S.
> Curtis?

EXT—DUTCH ROAD

Parked and nearly hidden in the circles of tree shadows is a convoy of German military trucks, carrying troops and about a dozen tanks. The convoy stretches for a quarter mile.

> MIKE O.S.
> The tree shadows on the road, sir.

INT/EXT—DODGE'S P-47

Dodge stares down at the convoy.

DODGE
          Holy crap! Sitting ducks, great eye, Mike! We'll
          split into pairs and work the road from oppo-
          site ends. Red Three take the sea end.

INT/EXT—PAUL'S P-47

Paul peels off toward the sea.

                              PAUL
          Red Three, roger!

EXT—SKY

Mike shadows Paul toward sea. Dodge and Jake dive inland.

INT/EXT—MIKE'S P-47

Mike dive bombs with Paul toward truck convoy.

                              PAUL O.S.
          Hate to interrupt their lunch hour. Let'er rip!

Paul dives and drops his bombs, Mike follows.

EXT—ROAD

Bombs explode almost simultaneously at both ends of convoy.

INT/EXT—MIKE'S P-47

Mike, paired with Paul, starts firing, strafing the road.

EXT—ROAD

The streams of bullets begin hitting the tanks and trucks. EXPLOSIONS, troops running from the trucks into the fields, many wounded, some vehicles on fire.

INT/EXT—JAKE'S P-47

Jake grins, following Dodge, and fires his guns and scores on trucks and tanks, EXPLOSIONS.

EXT—ROAD

The planes pass on opposite sides and come back again. Much of the convoy is in flames. German troops fire handguns, rifles, and machine guns at the fighters.

INT/EXT—MIKE'S P-47

Mike strafes behind Paul. Small arms fire PINGS off Eagle Eye. A shell chips the canopy near his face.

>   DODGE O.S.
>   Small arms fire, we'll make one more pass. Good
>   work!

EXT—ROAD

The fighters strafe the road again. The convoy is in shambles, on fire, disabled. Troops seek cover.

>   DODGE O.S.
>   All right, Red Flight, good day's work, let's head
>   for home.

The fighters fly toward the Dutch coast and the Channel.

EXT—LAWN—OFFICER'S CLUB—LATE AFTERNOON

Mike plays with Shep, throwing him a ball. Mike waves to Margret, as she pulls up in her Uncle's Land Rover.

Mike let's Shep in the backseat. Mike gets in the front.

EXT—OXBRIDGE AIRBASE

Margret drives out the gate and follows the road to her Uncle's nearby adjoining estate lands.

INT—CAR

From the backseat, Shep sticks his long nose into the front seat, getting between Mike and Margret.

>   MARGRET
>   Isn't the Base safe for Shep?

>   MIKE
>   He's a good boy, aren't you?
>   (to Margret)
>   Uhmmm, not exactly. The guys are calling him
>   the Dog of Death.

                              MARGRET
Oh dear, why?

                              MIKE
His first owner was a pilot who was killed, then his roommate fed him and he was killed, that crash you saw recently. It's a stupid superstition, and guys panicked.

                              MARGRET
Ah, that's a shame, poor thing.

She blows a kiss at Shep.

                              MARGRET (Cont., to Mike)
You're losing a lot of pilots, aren't you?

                              MIKE
Even one is too many.

                              MARGRET
The Germans are waiting for the invasion. You can feel it coming?

                              MIKE
It's coming. But the Germans don't know where we'll pour across.

                              MARGRET
What do you think?

                              MIKE
I don't know. I'm a line pilot, and I've got less than two hundred hours left on my tour. If I'm still here and able-bodied, it'll be great to be in on the invasion.

                              MARGRET
Great? That's an odd thing to say.

                              MIKE
Why?

                              MARGRET
It sounds like a sport, a game.

                                    MIKE
           No, it's no game.

EXT—PRIVATE ROAD TO THE WILLOWS

Just beyond the base the car turns off and enters a drive that leads to a carriage house within sight of the road, the lawn covered with willow trees, a small pond nearby. In the distance is an old Georgian mansion.

                                    MARGRET O.S.
           Well, fortunately I'm spending a lot of time
           here at The Willows. I can't concentrate in my
           college digs, too many distractions.

                                    MIKE O.S.
           This is like a slice of heaven. Shep you'll love it
           here.

The car stops and they emerge; Shep runs circles around Thomas Stanford, who strolls up with his walking stick. He takes to Shep immediately. Mike shakes hands with Stanford.

INT—COTTAGE LIVINGROOM—DAY

Robert Berksrun sits on the sofa flipping through papers filled with statistics. Margret enters with Shep and Mike and her uncle. Robert stands.

                                    ROBERT
           Hello Margret.

                                    MARGRET
           Oh, Robert!

Shep growls.

                                    STANFORD (to Shep)
           Pipe down there. He's already protecting you,
           Margret. Hello Robert.

                                    ROBERT
           Hello, sir. Sorry I didn't call, I had to rush up
           today. I've got that research you asked for,
           Margret, and I need to go over it.

> MARGRET
>
> Oh dear, you're going back to London today?
>
> ROBERT
>
> Sorry, yes.
>
> MARGRET
>
> Well, I'll have to drive Mike to the base first.
>
> MIKE
>
> No, no, I'll walk. It's a beautiful day. You do your work.
>
> MARGRET
>
> Oh dear.
>
> STANFORD
>
> I'll walk with you part way, Mike.
> (to Margret)
> I'll take Shep and show him about.

Shep leads the way out.

> ROBERT (to Mike)
>
> I'm sorry, old man, I hate to ruin your afternoon.
>
> MIKE
>
> No problem, I'll see Margret at the dance this weekend.
>
> MARGRET
>
> Yes, that's right.

Margret escorts them to the door.

> MIKE
>
> Goodbye til Saturday and thanks for taking Shep.
>
> MARGRET
>
> It's nothing. Anyway, I need a loyal protector. Goodbye, Mike, be careful.

Smiling, she closes the door and turns with a solemn, weary expression to face Robert. Robert opens a diary-like book toward her and smiles proudly.

                    ROBERT
      I've received the wireless codes. I'll need help
      with the transpositions, they're in German.

EXT—THE WILLOWS—DAY

Mike separates from Stanford and Shep and walks toward the road to the base. Stanford and Shep walk toward the mansion. A squadron of fighters takes off in the distance.

EXT—BRITISH COAST—DUSK—LATER

A large estate home overlooks the sea. Lights are on in some of the rooms. Military cars are parked in front. Overhead fighter planes cross the Channel.

INT/EXT—BEDROOM—ESTATE—DUSK

Ab sits at a desk near a window overlooking the sea. He's writing a letter.

                    AB V.O.
      So, you guys, I'll see you in a week or so, the food's
      great, and hey, keep the Grim Reaper intact.

Ab stops and stares at the planes DRONING over the sea. His writing hand starts shaking and he can't control it. He grabs the letter and crushes it and gasps for air.

EXT—SKY—PARIS, FRANCE—DAY

Within sight of Paris, Red Flight and other P-47s engage in high-flying dog fights with German fighters.

INT/EXT—JAKE'S P-47

Jake downs a German fighter, and does thumbs up in triumph.

                    JAKE
      Yeah! Number four!

INT/EXT—MIKE'S P-47

Mike is in a 360 degree-circle chasing a German fighter. Scores direct hits, and the German plane starts smoking. Pilot bails out, plane explodes. Mike dives to dodge debris and by accident his bomb rack clips the German's parachute. Mike banks and looks back grimly.

EXT—SKY/GROUND BELOW—DAY

The German pilot spirals rapidly to earth.

EXT—SKY—NEAR PARIS—DAY

Dodge has two ME-109s on his tail; one ME-109 is on Jake.

INT/EXT—PAUL'S P-47

Paul looks toward Dodge.

                                                PAUL
            Red Leader break left!

Paul and Mike dive toward German fighters.

INT/EXT—MIKE'S P-47

Mike looks ahead and sees the action.

                                                MIKE
                  On our way.

INT/EXT—PAUL'S P-47

German fighters dead ahead.

                                                PAUL
           I'll take the one on the left!

                                            MIKE O.S.
            I'll take the right one!

EXT—SKY—HIGHER ALTITUDE

Paul and Jake's planes almost collide. Red Leader (Dodge) dives into a cloud bank, followed by a German fighter.

EXT—SKY—LOWER ALTITUDE

Paul and Jake jockey in the chase after the two ME-109s. One of the 109's rolls over and heads for the deck.

Mike climbs for the cloud bank where Dodge disappeared.

INT/EXT—JAKE'S P-47

Jake grits his teeth and accelerates, lines up a shot on the remaining 109, and takes it, too far away.

                                                JAKE
          Back off, Paul, this one's mine.

INT/EXT—PAUL'S P-47

Paul takes aim, leads the fighter and starts firing.

                              PAUL
          You're lagging, gotta lead him.

The German flies through the shelling and the canopy explodes, fire erupts and the fuselage disintegrates.

                              JAKE O.S.
          You sonofabitch!

                              PAUL
          Ha!

                              JAKE O.S.
          Where's Mike?

                              PAUL
          Where's the Colonel, he's yours?

INT/EXT—JAKE'S P-47

Jake pulls up, looking around desperately.

                              PAUL O.S.
          Red Leader, this is Red Three.

INT/EXT—PAUL'S P-47

Radio CRACKLES. Sweating, Paul looks all around, sees Jake, but no Mike or Colonel.

                              PAUL
          Red Leader report, Mike?

INT/EXT—MIKE'S P-47

Mike flies through the cloud bank and finally breaks out.

                              PAUL/JAKE O.S.
          Red Flight, report.

                              MIKE
          This is Red Four, I'm across the river, no sight
          of Lead, no chutes.

EXT—SKY NEAR PARIS—LATER

The three P-47s circle and re-form in battle formation.

> MIKE O.S.
> Five more minutes, let's push it.

> PAUL O.S.
> We're low on fuel!

> JAKE O.S.
> Red Leader's been pushing his luck. This is his second tour and—

> PAUL O.S.
> Shut up, Jake, or I'll file on you.

> JAKE O.S.
> For what?

> MIKE O.S.
> He was your man, Jake.

> JAKE O.S.
> Mike followed him into that cloud.

> PAUL O.S.
> We're heading in, knock it off.

Paul's plane banks away from Paris, Jake and Mike follow.

EXT—HANGARS—OXBRIDGE AIRBASE—DUSK

Mike, Paul, and Jake, and other pilots look skyward as night falls; they stand in front of Mike's plane. Crew Chief Sandy George behind them pulls loose a strip of parachute silk wrapped around the bomb rack on Eagle Eye.

> SANDY (to Mike)
> Hey, here's a souvenir, Lieutenant!

> MIKE
> I don't want it, poor devil.

> JAKE
> Hell, I saw that *unfortunate* accident, Eagle Eye. I'll take it, keep it for good luck.

                                    MIKE
            Damn, where's Colonel Dodge?

Others shake their heads. A PILOT jogs by and stops.

                                    PILOT
            Hey, the show's about to start.

                                    PAUL
            I've got to find Edith.

                                    JAKE
            Lauren.

                                    MIKE
            Margret, I'm not up for this.

                                    PAUL
            Come on, hope for the best.

Jake shakes his head pessimistically, and they trudge off.

EXT—BASE HANGAR—NIGHT

Pilots and other servicemen loiter by the outside door. From inside BOB HOPE delivers a joke…

                                    HOPE O.S.
            Bing'll be along later, he's was delayed…He's in
            Jack Benny's vault counting all his money…

Laughter…Mike and Paul hurry into the building.

INT—BASE HANGAR

Mike and Paul work through the crowd. On the stage is Bob Hope and FRANCIS LANGFORD and musicians.

Paul spots Edith and Margret and points to them. He and Mike work their way to the two women.

                                    MIKE
            Hello, we were delayed.

                                    MARGRET
            I'm sorry about your Colonel, that's too bad.

Mike shakes his head sadly.

INT—ON STAGE

Jake, along with other U.S.O. officials, including Lauren, approach Hope and Langford with a trophy.

> JAKE
> On behalf of the personnel at this fine establishment, Bob and Francis, a little memento of your visit to Oxbridge, and many thanks.

Lauren hands hefty plaques inscribed on polished large shell casings to Hope and Langford.

> HOPE
> Thank you, it's been a pleasure.

> LANGFORD
> Oh, how nice.

Hope tests the weight of the plaque, goofs around as if it's too heavy, like a missile or bomb.

> HOPE
> Say, if I see any Nazis on the way to our next show, would you mind?

Audience roars with approval and laughter.

> HOPE
> Listen, you guys and gals, keep up the good work, we're praying for you. See you in Berlin!

The music comes up and Langford blows a kiss. APPLAUSE from audience. Jake leans into microphone.

> JAKE
> Dance commences immediately, folks.

A space is cleared in middle of hangar. The BAND begins to play, couples start dancing.

INT—DANCE FLOOR

Paul and Edith start dancing. Mike and Margret watch.

PAUL

Come on, you two!

Mike looks at Margret and takes her hand and leads her onto the floor, and they start dancing tentatively.

In the background, a V-1 ROCKET ENGINE can be heard over the MUSIC. The dancers stop and then the Band quiets, the ROCKET passes over, the Band plays again, the dancers dancing again. Margret draws closer to Mike.

INT—DANCE FLOOR—LATER

The Band is playing. Mike is dancing with Margret.

MIKE

How's Shep doing?

MARGRET

Oh he's like an old chum following Uncle around the estate.

MIKE

Great. I knew Shep was special.

Jake and Lauren approach. Jake taps Mike.

JAKE

Mind if we switch?

Mike hesitates. Lauren smiles at Mike.

MIKE

Sure.

JAKE

Now that's a southern gentleman.

Mike dances with Lauren, Jake with Margret. Mike is quiet with Lauren, but sees Jake talking rapidly with Margret.

LAUREN

Don't mind, Jake, he flirts with everyone.

MIKE

You don't mind?

                              LAUREN
            I've seen quite a few Jakes come through
            Oxbridge.

                              MIKE
            Oh yeah, how do they do?

                              LAUREN
            They take care of themselves.

                              MIKE
            Yeah, I can believe that, and how do the Mike
            types do?

Lauren hesitates.

                              MIKE (Cont.)
            Well?

Lauren forces a smile.

                              LAUREN
            Mikes take it all too seriously, so they don't
            sleep well. After they're gone home again, it's
            like they were never here.

                              MIKE
            Thank god!

Lauren laughs at Mike's bluntness. Mike looks around the room. Margret and Jake are nowhere in sight.

                              MIKE
            Let's step out for a smoke.

                              LAUREN
            Sure.

EXT—OUTSIDE HANGAR—NIGHT

Jake sits with Margret; they're smoking. Mike and Lauren approach. Jake uses his hands to describe an aerial battle.

                              JAKE
            I'd say we've got superior aircraft, and with the
            new P-51s coming on—

> MARGRET
>
> But how will you train for them?
>
> JAKE
>
> It's no—well, look who's here.
>
> MIKE
>
> Mind if we join you?

Jake waves them to a seat.

> MIKE (to Margret)
>
> It's called cross-training, switching to the P-51 from the Thunderbolts. It's done in stages.
>
> MARGRET
>
> Won't you be able to fly further with this new plane?
>
> MIKE
>
> Absolutely.
>
> JAKE
>
> Twice as far, and much faster.

Suddenly soldiers are running here and there. An MP, leading a German shepard guard dog, jogs by.

> JAKE
>
> Hey, what's up? Any word on Dodge?
>
> SOLDIER
>
> No, we're closing the base, threat of German paratroopers tonight.
>
> JAKE
>
> Not that again!

Paul and Edith come out.

> MIKE (to Paul)
>
> Base shutdown again.
>
> PAUL
>
> Oh hell!

MIKE (to Margret)
Sorry.

MARGRET
Is it a real threat?

MIKE
You never know, you may be Sprechen Sie Deutsch by morning.

MARGRET
I'm not that eager!

LAUREN (to women)
I'll drive everyone home.

Dancers are pouring out of the hangar, saying goodbye. Jake and Paul say goodbye to their dates.

MIKE (to Margret)
I want to see you again.

MARGRET
Yes, call me when you're free. We'll get together, just the two of us, this time.

MIKE
That sounds nice, until then.

MARGRET
Be careful up there.

Mike looks up at the night sky and nods in agreement.

EXT—BASE GATES—NIGHT—LATER

Soldiers close the gates. Searchlights sweep the skies. Nothing appears but low, roiling clouds.

INT—BEDROOM—THE WILLOWS—MIDNIGHT

A secret compartment is open, revealing a short wave radio and code transmitter. Margret and Robert are hunched over the radio, Robert with the maps of Europe, Margret tapping out code, haltingly, using the code book.

EXT—OXBRIDGE AIR BASE—DAWN

P-47s crank up and taxi down the runways. They take off, four abreast into the inclement weather.

EXT—SKY—DAWN

The fighters join the bombers and off they go for Germany.

EXT—SKY—LATER

Flak begins puffing around the lead bombers and fighters. One bomber is hit and catches fire. Several bombers feather engines and turn back. A squadron of fighters replaces the squadron from Oxbridge.

INT/EXT—PAUL'S P-47

Paul looks out at the replacement fighters.

> PAUL
> Okay, guys, here's our replacements, it's all yours.

Paul looks over at Mike, Jake and others.

INT/EXT—MIKE'S P-47

Mike waves to Paul, checks his fuel gauge. Flak explodes nearby, jolting his plane. Mike turns back toward the English Channel.

INT/EXT—JAKE'S P-47

Jake waves the piece of German parachute at Paul and ties it to his instrument panel.

> JAKE
> Onward, Musketeers!

Jake follows Paul's lead.

EXT—SKY—HOLLAND—MORNING

The Oxbridge pilots fly toward the English Channel.

INT/EXT—MIKE'S P-47

Mike scans the Dutch coast through the cloud cover.

EXT—THIN CLOUDS—SKY

A B-17 Fortress, its engines smoking slightly, circles.

INT/EXT—MIKE'S P-47

Mike cranes for a better view.

                        MIKE
    A Big Friend in trouble, six o'clock, ten thousand
    feet, Red Leader?

                        PAUL O.S.
    Roger, let's take a look.

EXT—SKY

Paul, followed by Jake, Mike and fourth pilot (sub for Ab), and several other fighters, dive toward the circling bomber.

EXT—BOMBER—SKY

The fighters circle the slowly circling bomber. Three of the four engines are shutdown, slight trails of smoke issue from the other engine, the doors are open, no sign of a crew.

INT/EXT—MIKE'S P-47

Mike flies very close to the bomber and inspects the open doors, the insignia reads, "MISS BETTY BOOP."

                        PAUL O.S.
    Betty Boop, are you there? Betty Boop, come in.

INT/EXT—PAUL'S P-47

Paul stares at the bomber.

                        PAUL
    There's nobody at the controls. Any sign of chutes?

INT/EXT—JAKE'S P-47

Jake banks his plane and surveys the ground.

                        JAKE
    No chutes.

INT/EXT—MIKE'S P-47

Mike tries to get closer.

                              MIKE
          Looks abandoned from here.

                              JAKE O.S.
          Let's shoot it down.

                              PAUL O.S.
          No! Somebody could be on board, injured maybe.

                              JAKE O.S.
          Gonna die anyway.

                              MIKE
          It won't count for your ace, Jake.

INT/EXT—JAKE'S P-47

Jake shakes his finger at Mike.

                              JAKE
          That's a cheap shot.

                              MIKE O.S.
          Granted.

                              PAUL O.S.
          Okay you two, we'll call it in.

                              JAKE
          It's like that ghost bomber in Ab's dream, man,
          don't tell him about this…spooky…

INT/EXT—COCKPIT TO REAR—BOMBER

Down the interior, empty, wind whipping through.

EXT—OXBRIDGE AIRBASE—AFTERNOON

Raining. A bus stops and Mike jumps on. The bus travels a short distance along the narrow highway.

EXT—KING JOHN PUB—AFTERNOON

The King John Pub is next to the rail station to London. The bus stops and Mike and several other soldiers and civilians dismount. Mike enters the King John Pub.

INT—KING JOHN PUB

Mike joins Margret at a table. She's sipping a beer. A number of servicemen are present, watching them. Mike orders from the waitress.

                        MIKE
I didn't know it would be so noisy.

                        MARGRET
The rain boxes them in here.

There's loud laughter and a RADIO BLARES out music. Mike fidgets in his chair as the waitress brings him a beer.

                        MIKE (to waitress)
Thanks.

                        MARGRET
Uncomfortable, something wrong?

                        MIKE
I'm just tired.

                        MARGRET
How's Ab?

                        MIKE
He's due back in a couple of days.

Mike lights Margret's cigarette and lights one of his own. His hand shakes almost imperceptibly, but Margret notices.

                        MARGRET
Let's get out of here.

                        MIKE
Where?

                        MARGRET
The Willows. You can see Shep. I'll make us a pot of tea.

                        MIKE
God, that sounds nice.

                        MARGRET
Fine.

Margret looks around the room and spots BEATTY, an elderly taxi driver, propped at the bar.

                                              MARGRET

        Beatty?

                                              BEATTY

        Yes, Miss Toland?

                                              MARGRET

        A lift to The Willows?

Beatty doffs his cap.

                                              BEATTY

        At your service.

EXT—THE WILLOWS—AFTERNOON

Raining. The taxi pulls up to the house. Mike and Margret emerge, Mike blocks her from paying the fare.

                                              MARGRET

        You silly, don't waste your pay.

                                              MIKE

        Please, it makes me feel almost normal again.

Margret laughs.

                                              MARGRET

        Bye Beatty.

                                              BEATTY

        Bye bye, Miss Toland!

They run and stand under the eaves by the porch. They must stand close as she gets out her key. She smiles, Mike smiles. Shep can be heard WHIMPERING beyond the door.

                                              MIKE

        Hello Shep!

Shep BARKS in recognition. Margret opens the door and they enter, Shep dancing around.

MARGRET
I'll start the tea.

INT—THE WILLOWS—LATER

Mike and Margret sit by the fire in the fireplace and sip tea. Rain runs down the windows. Shep lies nearby.

MIKE
It's really relaxing here.

MARGRET
I've gotten a lot of work done at The Willows, it's so quiet.

A squadron of P-47s DRONES to life in the distance. Mike and Margret laugh.

MIKE
Except for the damned Yanks…

MARGRET
I don't mind. I'm glad you're here.

MIKE
Me?

MARGRET
Yes, you.

Margret smiles and picks up a cigarette and Mike lights a match. As he draws near her with the match, she blows out the match and moves closer. He kisses her gently. Their kissing advances. Margret stands and pulls him to his feet and draws him after her to the bedroom. Mike hesitates.

MIKE
You don't even know if I'm married.

MARGRET
Are you?

MIKE
No.

MARGRET
Engaged?

                          MIKE
No.

                          MARGRET
Serious girlfriend?

                          MIKE
No…nothing serious.

                          MARGRET
There's a war on, you know. Come along, what's the hesitation?

                          MIKE
I can't imagine.

Mike carefully shuts the bedroom door, blocking Shep who tries to follow.

                          MIKE (to Shep)
You're on guard duty, old man.

Shep whimpers.

INT—BEDROOM—THE WILLOWS—LATER

Margret's bedroom has large windows overlooking the pond and the road in the distance. The room is stacked with books and papers, clutter of clothes, a small telescope on a tripod near the window, and her hunting rifles over her desk.

Margret and Mike lie arm in arm after making love in the bed. The rain continues, the hush swallowing the house.

                          MARGRET
Better?

                          MIKE
Much better.

                          MARGRET
Tell me…what will you do after the war?

                          MIKE
I don't know…my Dad wants me to go to college and run the family drugstore one day…

MARGRET
I can't imagine you mixing potions all day in the rear of a chemist shop! What will you do, really?

MIKE
Well, there's an airfield outside of town. I thought of starting up a small repair service, maybe teach flying…maybe even run a short-hop service to Richmond and Washington.

MARGRET
Now that's more like you…
(kisses him)
And if you get bored in civilian aviation, you can always come back to Britain…we'll be having another war no doubt…

MIKE
This one will do, thank you, but I'll always want to come back to see you…

MARGRET
You southerners are such charmers…

Mike smiles slyly and kisses Margret passionately.

EXT—NEAR HANGAR—OXBRIDGE AIRBASE—MORNING

Ab, fresh from briefing with Red Flight, returns to his plane, the Grim Reaper, and shakes hands with his CREW CHIEF and OTHER MAINTENANCE PEOPLE.

Red Flight climbs in their planes and taxis for take-off.

EXT—RUNWAY

Take-off, flight after flight.

EXT—SKY—GERMANY—MORNING

Fighters escort bombers.

German fighters attack and U.S. pilots engage in dogfights.

A German fighter, aflame, spirals down from the skies.

Bomber crews take to their chutes as a bomber konks out.

Bombers drop their bombs on targets in Germany.

EXT—GROUND—GERMANY—MORNING

Bombs destroy industrial/train yards.

EXT—AERODROME—GERMANY—DAY

American pilots strafe an airfield, blowing up planes and buildings. Flak explodes around them.

One plane is hit and crashes on the field.

EXT—SKY—ENGLISH CHANNEL—DAY

A bomber loses altitude over the sea. The bomber ditches into the Channel.

Crews climb into rubber dinghies. Sea rescue ships approach.

EXT—HANGARS—OXBRIDGE—DUSK

Sandy George, and other crewchiefs, ground personnel and pilots, wait, watching the skies for returning planes.

Red Flight lands and Mike and the others taxi up.

INT/EXT—MIKE'S P-47—DUSK

Mike pencils his total hours on the instrument panel, 145.

INT—OFFICER'S CLUB—NIGHT

The officers stand in the memorial circle with lit candles. Mike, Ab, Paul and Jake watch as an OFFICER burns another name in the beams, "Lt. Whitman, 4-15-44."

INT/EXT—MIKE'S P-47—OVER FRANCE—DAY

Mike pulls behind a German fighter and blasts him; explosion—the pilot ejects and the plane spirals down.

INT/EXT—JAKE'S P-47—OVER FRANCE—DAY

Jake fires ahead of a German fighter and the plane crosses into it and explodes. Jake gives a thumbs up.

                              JAKE
Bingo! That's five! Ace!

INT/EXT—AB'S P-47—OVER FRANCE—DAY

Ab strafes a train and hits the boiler of the locomotive. Steam shoots sky high.

INT/EXT—PAUL'S P-47—OVER FRANCE—DAY

Paul strafes a train yard and hits ammunition on the train cars. A terrific EXPLOSION. He pulls up just in time, debris flying around his plane. Paul crosses himself.

INT/EXT—MIKE'S P-47—AFTERNOON

Mike taxis to a stop and shuts down his plane. He looks at the latest combat total, 162, strikes it and writes, 167.

INT—OFFICER'S CLUB—NIGHT

The squadron assembles in the memorial circle, adds another name and date (Lt. Greely, 4-20-44) to the beams.

Ab swallows hard, his face pale, as he stands among Red Flight, all their faces creased with strain, sadness.

INT—LIVING ROOM—THE WILLOWS—NIGHT

Mike puts his finger to his lips, shushing Shep, as he backs into the bedroom with Margret. The door closes.

EXT—STANFORD'S ESTATE LANDS—EARLY A.M.

Foggy. Stanford, Robert, Margret and Mike advance four abreast with hunting rifles, stepping quietly through the meadows. A group of deer graze in the distance. Robert nods to Mike to take the shot.

INT/EXT—GUNSIGHT—MIKE'S RIFLE

Mike lines up the crosshairs on the buck but delays.

           ROBERT O.S.
  Fire, man!

Mike shifts the crosshairs slightly, aiming at a "Posted—Private Property" sign just above the buck's head. GUNSHOT.

EXT—MEADOW AND TREE

Sign flies off. Deer take flight.

EXT—HUNTERS

Robert takes quick aim and FIRES at fleeing deer. A doe goes down, wounded, thrashing in the high grass.

                         MARGRET
        Poor thing! Oh Robert—

                         ROBERT
        I'll fix it!

EXT—MEADOW

Robert runs up to the flailing deer. He pulls a revolver and SHOOTS it in the head. The others watch at a distance. Mike shakes his head regretfully as Margret and Stanford look on. Mike, with a farewell wave, turns and walks away.

EXT—HANGARS—OXBRIDGE—DUSK

Red Flight lands and taxis to their hangar area.

INT/EXT—MIKE'S P-47

Mike pencils in his latest combat total, 175, as Sandy pulls back his canopy.

EXT—DEBRIEFING—OPERATIONS—LATER

Mike and the other pilots walk slowly, exhausted, toward Debriefing Office. "Captain" Watson, recently promoted Intelligence Officer, grinning, cuts off the pilots.

                         WATSON
        Delay your debriefing for a few minutes! Step
        into Mission Planning, we've got a surprise.

INT—MISSION PLANNING ROOM

The pilots fill the briefing room. Capt. Watson and the new Commander stand in front of room.

                         COMMANDER
        Before you men pass through debriefing, we
        thought you'd like a chance to share a really
        happy moment for us all. Captain Watson, you
        do the honors.

> WATSON
> Thank you, sir, well, without further ado, gentlemen, please stand.

Everyone rises, Watson opens the door.

> WATSON (Cont.)
> Attenshunt!

Everyone comes to attention, as in marches Colonel Dodge, much thinner, limping.

> PILOTS
> Colonel Dodge!

INT—AUDIENCE

Mike, Paul, and Jake are grinning. Ab can't keep a smile, tears come to his eyes.

INT—STAGE—MISSION PLANNING

Dodge, emotional, gives a wave. The pilots shout approval and begin clapping.

> DODGE
> At ease, gentlemen! At ease!

The applause dies down and the pilots sit down. Dodge stands in front of the strategic maps and before a lectern.

> DODGE
> Thank you, it's good to be back. Unfortunately, I'll be moving on, reassigned to Mission Planning in London, and as you know, for security reasons, mostly to protect our resistance friends across the Channel, we don't want to risk any leaks should us returnees get shot down again, so my combat days are over at least in the ETO.

Paul raises his hand.

> DODGE
> Yes, Paul?

> PAUL
> Colonel, we're sorry about what happened.

                        DODGE
            Hey, I got my butt in a crack, there was nothing
            you guys could do, I'm not blaming you at all.

Jake sighs mightily. Mike swallows hard. An OFFICER down front raises his hand.

                        DODGE
            Yes?

                        OFFICER
            How'd you get back, sir?

                        DODGE
            The French Resistance, fantastic, great guys,
            and I came across the channel through the
            island of Guernsey, went like clockwork.

                        OFFICER
            How's it going for them, sir?

Dodge, frowning, glances at Capt. Watson on the podium.

                        DODGE
            Men, there's more bad news. Something's really
            gone wrong under the Nazis. Everywhere I went,
            the Resistance people are whispering about what
            the Nazis are doing to the Jews and the Gypsies,
            rounding them up, shipping them to concentra-
            tion camps, there's talk of mass extermination,
            people not returning, not coming back.

The room is perfectly still. Capt. Watson squirms uncomfortably on the podium, watching the men and Dodge.

                        DODGE (Cont.)
            Sadly, I learned that Lieutenant Steinmetz, who
            was initially listed as a POW, was classified as a
            Jew and removed to an unknown location inside
            Germany. His fate is unknown at this hour.

INT—AUDIENCE OF PILOTS

The pilots stare ahead, some blankly, thoughtfully, others shaking their heads in disgust.

INT—PODIUM

Dodge steps away from the podium.

                                  DODGE (Cont.)
        I've enjoyed leading you men. Believe me, you're doing the right thing here, there's something rotten in Denmark *and* in the heart of Germany, and we're here to root it out. God Bless you and keep you, goodbye for now.

Pilots rise and salute. Dodge salutes and exits the room.

INT—AUDIENCE OF PILOTS

Mike looks at Paul, Ab, and Jake.

                                  PAUL (to others)
        Lousy Krauts! I can't wait for the invasion!

                                  JAKE
        Let's hit the club for a few.

The others nod, Ab's face is pale, his eyes somewhat feverish. Mike looks grim.

EXT—RED LION—CAMBRIDGE—DAY

Mike is dropped off in a staff car in Cambridge.

INT—RED LION

Mike joins Margret in a booth. Mike pours himself a beer from a pitcher. Margret is smoking a cigarette. A stack of books and papers are on the table.

                                  MARGRET
        Hello darling, how are you?

She gives him a light kiss on the cheek.

                                  MIKE
        Miserable, frankly.

                                  MARGRET
        But I would think you'd be delighted, Colonel Dodge survived—

                              MIKE
The Germans are exterminating Jews.

                              MARGRET
No they're not.

                              MIKE
They're rounding them up and putting them to death.

                              MARGRET
No, they're relocating them, that's different.

                              MIKE
You don't seem to hear me. Dodge said the resistance fighters—

                              MARGRET
Consider the source, Mike.

                              MIKE
You say the Germans are the most educated people on earth? And this is happening?

Margret crushes out her cigarette. Across the room, Jake comes in with several other pilots who line up at the bar.

                              MARGRET
Look, you're naive about European warfare. This is nothing new.

                              MIKE
Extermination?

                              MARGRET
Relocation! There's a difference.

                              MIKE
I'm telling you—

Jake appears at the table. He's drunk.

                              JAKE
Don't believe a word he says.

MIKE (to Jake)
Do you mind?

JAKE
Excuse me, I didn't know this was serious.

MARGRET
It's not—

MIKE
It damned well is!

JAKE
What?

MARGRET
The European Jewish question. Mike doesn't want to hear this is an old thing in Europe, anti-Semitism, for God's sake, your own country is rampantly anti-Jewish, anti-Negro, anti-Indian.

JAKE
She's got a point. We relocated the Indians, didn't we? Heard of the Trail of Tears? Or the slave trade?

Mike stands up.

MARGRET
You're leaving? I thought—

MIKE
I'll take a rain check on The Willows.

Mike looks at her, she at him for a moment. Jake observes. Mike walks out. Jake and Margret watch him go.

MARGRET
Dammit!

JAKE
He's an innocent, a small town guy, what do you expect?

Margret picks up another cigarette. Jake slides into the booth and lights it.

JAKE (Cont.)
So, tell me about The Willows.

MARGRET
God, you Yanks are brassy.

JAKE
Uh huh, at your service.

MARGRET
Don't you have a mission?

JAKE
All too soon, my dear...

INT—BARRACKS—NIGHT

Mike lies awake in his bed. Paul and Ab sleep, Ab fitfully, muttering incoherently. Jake comes in and bumbles about in the dark of the bedroom. He spots Mike awake.

JAKE
Nice place, The Willows, but the mattress is a bit soft!

MIKE
Kiss my ass.

JAKE
Listen you greenhorn, she's bad medicine, you know what I mean?

Mike leaps up and grabs Jake by the collar.

MIKE
I'm sick of you, Russell!

Jake takes a drunken swing at Mike. They wrestle to the floor, grunting and groaning. Paul and Ab jump out of bed and pull them apart. Mike and Jake face each other, held back by the two men. Two PILOTS look in the room.

PILOT
What the hell!

PAUL
It's nothing, nothing!

EXT—RUNWAY—OXBRIDGE—DAWN

A flight of P-47s takes off, and one plane, overloaded, crashes in the woods beyond the revetments.

EXT—AERODROME—FRANCE—DAY

P-47s strafe aerodromes. Flak is heavy. One P-47 takes a direct hit, exploding, crashing.

EXT—SKY—FRANCE—DAY

P-47s engage in dog-fighting German fighters.

German fighter takes hits, pilot ejects, plane explodes.

EXT—ENGLISH CHANNEL—DAY

A P-47 crashes into the sea.

EXT—COASTAL BASE—ENGLAND—DAY

P-47 crash lands on emergency runway on the English coast.

INT—OFFICER'S CLUB—NIGHT

The pilots perform the candle ceremony in memory of another dead pilot, the name "Lt. Darwin, 5-1-44" goes on roofbeam.

EXT—RUNWAY—OXBRIDGE—DUSK

Flights of P-47s land and taxi toward hangars. Several planes arrive with major damage.

A wounded pilot is lifted from one P-47; blood covers his flight suit.

One P-47 lands, taxis, catches fire. Firetrucks spray the plane as rescue crewmen haul out the stunned pilot.

EXT—HANGAR—OXBRIDGE—NIGHT

Repair crews work on damaged planes.

Ammo specialists load up planes for more missions.

INT—DINING ROOM—OFFICERS—NIGHT

Pilots are standing in prayer. They sit down, leaving several empty seats, their chairs tipped forward. Ab remains standing, staring at the empty chairs. Mike, Paul, and Jake look at Ab. Paul pulls his sleeve and he takes his seat.

EXT—HANGAR AREA—DAY

Mike, other pilots, and Sandy George and crew chiefs, are looking over a new P-51. They have the radio on in the new plane and hear the TOWER-TO-PILOT TRANSMISSIONS. They hear LT. KEARNS on the radio from a P-47 in flight near Oxbridge.

> KEARNS O.S.
> Oxbridge Tower, this is Test Flight Beta, five miles south of the field, 5,000 feet. I'm losing power and altitude, declaring an emergency…

> TOWER O.S.
> Roger, Test Flight, we're holding take-offs, bring her in.

> SANDY
> Oh hell, that's that sorry hangar queen we've been trying to patch up. What a jinx! I told Kearns to forget it!

Everyone jumps off the P-51 and scrambles for a better view.

INT/EXT—KEARNS' P-47

Kearns struggles to keep the power up, the plane on the flight path to the runway.

EXT—AIRBASE ROAD

Along the road comes Thomas Stanford, driving his car.

INT—CAR

Stanford HUMS a tune, Shep curled on the floor. Shep cocks his ear, Stanford glances to his right, sees something.

INT/EXT—KEARNS' P-47

Kearns, a silent scream, rears back in shocked horror.

EXT—AIRBASE ROAD

Kearns' P-47 sheers off the cab of Stanford's Land Rover and the plane crash lands near the runway's end in a meadow.

The plane explodes into flames.

Mike and airbase personnel run up the road.

EXT/INT—CAR

Mike looks in the car. Stanford has been decapitated. Mike looks away.

Mike hears a whimper. He peers in and sees Shep cowering in the wreckage. Mike helps Shep from the wreckage, petting it.

> JAKE
> Man, this is scary, it's that damned dog again.

Ab and Paul look on grimly.

> MIKE (to Jake)
> Shut up!
> (to Shep)
> It's okay, boy, it's okay.

EXT—FIELD

Kearns' P-47 burns, ammunition explodes. Firetrucks arrive and spray it with jets of water and foam.

EXT—OLD ENGLISH CEMETERY—DAY

Mike and other pilots stand with crowd at graveside service for Stanford. Margret has a face of grim, tearless resolve. Next to her is Robert Berksrun.

An Episcopal PRIEST finishes a prayer, the mourners start to leave. Berksrun escorts her toward a car. Mike and Jake step toward her.

> MIKE
> Margret, I'm very sorry.

Margret looks at him briefly without emotion and moves on, but Mike starts to follow. Jake waits with a wry smile.

> ROBERT (to Mike)
> Not now, Lieutenant, another time.

Robert climbs in the car with Margret. The door shuts and the car pulls away.

> JAKE (to Paul)
> He'll never learn he's not welcome.

                                              PAUL
          Shut up, Jake.

INT—OFFICER'S CLUB—NIGHT

Pilots perform the candle ceremony and etch Kearns' name in the rafters (5-9-44). Mike hangs his head, unable to watch.

EXT—REVIEWING STAND—RUNWAY—DAY

Old P-47s and new P-51s are parked in rows before the reviewing stand. The pilots and crews stand before the planes. On the reviewing stand are the military brass and local visitors, including Margret (in mourning), Edith and Lauren. Also present is middle-aged Captain EDDIE RICKENBACKER. A top Air Corps GENERAL stands at the podium.

                                           GENERAL
                    I want to thank our visitors again for being with
                    us, and Captain Eddie Rickenbacker, our top
                    ace in World War One…Now Captain, if you
                    will join me, we'll present the Distinguished
                    Flying Crosses and other awards.

EXT—RED FLIGHT—DAY

Jake's P-47 is next to Mike's plane. The General and Rickenbacker, accompanied by AIDES, move down the line, awarding DFC's to Ab and Paul.

Then they come to Jake and his ground crew behind him.

                                           GENERAL
          Lieutenant Jake Russell—

                                              JAKE
          Yes sir.

Jake salutes smartly, and they return his salute.

                                           GENERAL
                    I want to congratulate you on your fifth enemy
                    plane destroyed. You have now achieved the
                    status of an ace. Congratulations.

                                              JAKE
          Thank you, sir.

> GENERAL
> And further, in recognition of your leadership and general contribution to morale through your outstanding performance, we present you with the Distinguished Flying Cross and, not least, your double bars. Congratulations, Captain.

General pins on DFC and Captain's bars.

> RICKENBACKER
> Congratulations, Captain.

> JAKE
> Thank you, sir, it's a great honor to meet.

> RICKENBACKER
> Careful now, you don't break my kill record.

> JAKE
> Twenty-six aircraft! Not a chance, sir.

EXT—MIKE'S P-47—REVIEWING AREA—DAY

The General and Rickenbacker come to Mike.

> GENERAL
> Lieutenant Curtis, congratulations on your fourth confirmed kill. In recognition of your accomplishments to date, you are hereby awarded the Distinguished Flying Cross.

> MIKE
> Thank you, sir.

While the General pins on the medal, Rickenbacker looks at the Eagle Eye insignia on side of the plane.

> GENERAL
> Congratulations, Lieutenant Curtis.

> MIKE
> Thank you, sir.

Mike shakes hands with the General and Rickenbacker. They start away and suddenly Rickenbacker turns back to whisper.

                              RICKENBACKER
Curtis…you're the Virginian with the Stearman,
aren't you?

                              MIKE
Yes sir…

                              RICKENBACKER
We biplane pilots had an old sayin' in the
Great War, works anytime.

                              MIKE
Yes sir?

                              RICKENBACKER
Fly high and keep your nose in the wind.

                              MIKE
That's good, I'll remember that, sir, thank you.

Rickenbacker winks and hustles after the GENERAL.

Mike looks at Jake, preening over his new Captain's bars. Jake grins at Mike and gives him the Victory sign. Then Jake blows a kiss at the reviewing stand.

EXT—REVIEWING STAND—DAY

Both Margret and Lauren start to return blown kisses and suddenly see each other in the same motion, smile primly.

EXT—MIKE'S P-47—DAY

Mike watches the women in the stands and mutters—

                              MIKE
Fly high and keep your nose in the wind.

EXT—GATE—OXBRIDGE—LATER

Jake and Margret ride away in a car toward The Willows. Mike watches them go and almost starts walking after them.

                              LAUREN (to Mike)
Mike!

Mike turns around.

                              LAUREN (Cont.)
            Come with us, won't you?

Lauren nods toward Paul who's talking with Ab and Edith.

                              LAUREN (Cont.)
            We're going to King John's.

Mike hesitates, looks down the road at the disappearing car, then walks with Lauren to the group. A staff car pulls up and they climb in. Ab stands outside, his DFC medal shining on his uniform.

                              PAUL (to Ab)
            Come on! Have a beer!

                              AB
            No, I need some sleep.

Mike motions him in, but Ab shakes his head adamantly. The car pulls away. Everyone waves goodbye, Ab waves wearily.

EXT—OXBRIDGE AIRBASE—DAY—SECONDS LATER

A B-17 buzzes the airbase. Ab looks up. Personnel everywhere look up at the low-flying bomber. Two corpsman walk by Ab.

                              CORPSMAN#1 (to #2)
            Who's that show off?

                              CORPSMAN#2
            Some joyriding clown!

Ab starts toward the barracks, changes his mind, starts back across road to hangar area.

EXT—RUNWAY—OXBRIDGE—LATER

The B-17 lands and taxis up to the hangars. The insignia on the side reads "Lucky Lady," with a Vargas girl pinup. Ab is nearby, inspecting his P-47.

A small crowd gathers around the cockpit of the B-17. Ab joins them. The pilot James Tubbs leans out of the window.

                              TUBBS
            We're looking for a local hero.

GROUNDMAN
Who's that?

TUBBS
Curtis, Lieutenant Mike Curtis.

AB
I know him.

TUBBS
We owe him a little liquid refreshment and a free flight in Lucky Lady here.

AB
Just missed him, he went to King John's Pub down the road there.

TUBBS
Oh yeah.

AB
Yeah.

TUBBS
You know the way?

AB
Sure.

TUBBS
Hop in, we'll give him a surprise.

Ab looks at the bomber, propellers revving, and hesitates.

TUBBS (Cont.)
Come on, man, I don't have long. Say, there's a fifth in it for you.

SANDY GEORGE (to Ab)
Ah, go ahead, Lieutenant.

AB
Well, I've always wanted to try one of these crates, safety in numbers.

                                    TUBBS
            Now's your chance. Anybody else? Back in fif-
            teen minutes.

Several other pilots and crewmen, including Sandy, Mike's Crew Chief, climb inside for the ride.

INT/EXT—B-17 BOMBER

The bomber crew welcomes them aboard. There are several cases of Scotch the crew with marks for the officer's and NCO clubs. Ab climbs into the cockpit with Tubbs and the CO-PILOT. Everyone laughs and they taxi for take-off.

EXT—RUNWAY

Lucky Lady takes off.

EXT—STAFF CAR—KING JOHN PUB—LATER

Mike, Lauren, Edith, and Paul walk from the car to pub. Behind the pub a passenger train starts to pull away.

                                    PAUL
            I'm down to my last forty hours.

                                    EDITH
            Don't talk about it, it's bad luck.

                                    PAUL
            Okay, okay.

A bomber's engine DRONE can be heard coming closer.

                                    LAUREN
            What's that?!

                                    MIKE
            Four engines—

Lucky Lady BOOMS right over them.

EXT—LUCKY LADY

The crew's waving, the insignia in full sight.

EXT—KING JOHN

The foursome ducks involuntarily.

                    MIKE

Lucky Lady—

                    PAUL

Hey isn't that—

                    MIKE

Yeah, those guys last month? Seems like a year ago.

                    PAUL

Ab was in the waist window!

                    MIKE

So that's why Ab stayed back?

                    LAUREN

What did you *do* to those guys?

                    MIKE

Nothing! I escorted them back from a mission over Germany.

                    LAUREN

Are they happy?

                    MIKE

I hope so!

                    PAUL

Oh hell, here they come again.

EXT—RAILWAY LINE

The bomber is flying very low, coming across the tracks, passing over the departing train. The smoke from the train sweeps over the fuselage of the plane.

                    MIKE O.S.

Damn that's low!

                    PAUL O.S.

Holy Jesus!

INT/EXT—LUCKY LADY COCKPIT

Tubbs, with Ab and others crouched behind the pilot and co-pilot, react with horror as they jolt downward, windshield obscured by smoke.

EXT—RAILWAY LINE

The bomber hits the tree tops, drops suddenly and disappears behind a copse of trees. There's a momentary quiet, then a terrific EXPLOSION. A fireball rises beyond the trees.

EXT—KING JOHN PUB

Mike and Paul run down the road, leaving the women. Other soldiers from the pub follow them. One man runs for a phone.

EXT—FIELD

The bomber is burning fiercely, EXPLOSIONS wrack its fuselage. The heat is so intense, Mike, Paul and other soldiers can only stand at a distance and watch in horror.

INT—OFFICER'S DINING HALL—NIGHT

The candle ceremony is held again. Paul etches Ab's name and date of death (5-20-44). A number of candles burn on their ladders commemorating the multiple losses.

Mike watches in the circle of solemn pilots. Doc Lewis studies Mike and Paul.

EXT—STEPS—OFFICER'S CLUB—NIGHT

The pilots leave the club. Mike stops on the steps and looks up at the night sky. Jake and Paul stop nearby and look up.

                              JAKE
Just got the word from the Colonel.

                              PAUL
Yeah?

                              JAKE
I'm going to London on TDY, start learning mission planning.

                              PAUL
You're off the line flying?

                              JAKE
Hell no! I'll be back soon.

Doc Lewis steps outside and comes over to the threesome.

                    DOC

    Paul, Mike, you guys are on R and R, the south of England for ten days—

                    JAKE

    Good! They won't gain on my combat hour total, we'll still be going home together.

                    PAUL

    Oh come on, Doc, I'm down to forty hours. I just wanta finish up and get the hell outta here.

                    MIKE

    Me too.

                    JAKE

    Real troopers, aren't they!

Doc Lewis gives Jake a withering glance.

                    DOC

    No debate, no discussion. Your orders are cut.

Mike shakes his head in resignation.

                    DOC

    Play a little golf, chase some women, but above all, get some sleep. You guys look like hell.

                    MIKE

    That's where we've been, Doc.

Doc nods his head and walks away.

EXT—MANSION—S. ENGLAND—DAY

A car delivers Mike and Paul to the pilots rest home, a castle-like mansion of forty rooms. STAFF people welcome them and take their bags.

INT—FOYER—MANSION—DAY

Mike and Paul sign in. To one side is a billiards and card room. In the other direction is a library, a few PILOTS reading, writing letters. Very quiet atmosphere.

INT—HALLWAY—MANSION—DAY

Mike and Paul are escorted by a young STAFF WOMAN who shows them to their separate rooms.

INT—MIKE'S ROOM—DAY

Mike steps into his room, closes the door, and slumps in a chair. He lights a cigarette and stares out the window at the beautiful countryside.

EXT—MANSION GROUNDS—SUNSET

Mike and Paul walk over the grounds and stare out at the sunset from the terrace overlooking the meadows.

INT—MIKE'S ROOM—NIGHT

Mike twists and turns trying to sleep. He gets up and lights a cigarette, and paces the room.

INT—DININGROOM—MANSION—MORNING

Mike's reading a letter. Paul approaches him. Both men look more relaxed, rested.

                PAUL
What, less than a week and you're already getting fan mail?

                MIKE
Margret…wonder how she knew we were here?

                PAUL
Edith, no doubt.

                MIKE
She wants me to meet her in London.

                PAUL
Hey, you're supposed to be resting, old chum.

                MIKE
To hell with that.

                PAUL
I didn't hear a thing.

                                    MIKE
Thanks.

                                    PAUL
Say, you're looking better already.

                                    MIKE
I'll surprise her.

                                    PAUL
Just remember—

                                    MIKE
What?

                                    PAUL
If Jake's there—

                                    MIKE
Yeah, yeah, don't punch him out.

                                    PAUL
He outranks you now. Say, are you sure you didn't grow up on the streets of the North End?

                                    MIKE
Trust me.

INT/EXT—TRAIN—NEAR LONDON—DAY

Mike, reading the newspaper, rides in the train approaching London. He's dressed in a Class A uniform: military blouse, tie and trousers and cap; he wears his new DFC medal.

EXT—MISSION PLANNING BUILDING—LONDON—DAY

Security checks military people in and out of gate. Across the street a fancy car waits at the curb, Margret and Robert in the backseat, a DRIVER in front.

INT—MISSION PLANNING ROOM

Over a giant model of England and Europe officers position miniature fighters and bombers with long sticks across the corridor toward Berlin.

Jake stands with a group, including Colonel Dodge, listing squadron assignments on boards. He glances at his watch.

                                    JAKE
            Damn, I'm late!

Jake dashes out.

EXT—TRAIN STATION—LONDON—DAY

Mike leaves the station and hails a cab.

EXT—TOWNHOUSES—LONDON—DAY

The taxi pulls over at a corner in a wealthy townhouse neighborhood in London. The streets are busy with people and vehicles. Mike climbs out.

He looks around glancing at the numbers on the houses and the letter in his hand. He finds the house and starts up the stairs, but hesitates. He glances about and spots a pub nearby on the commercial sidestreet. He walks toward it, The Pewter Pint.

INT/EXT—PEWTER PINT—DAY—LATER

Mike stands at the bar near the window where he glances out at Margret's townhouse. He finishes his first beer and accepts his second mug from the silver-haired BARTENDER.

EXT—TOWNHOUSE—DAY

The fancy car seen earlier pulls up to the townhouse.

INT/EXT—PEWTER PINT

Mike takes another quick swallow and digs for the money.

                                    BARTENDER
            On the house, sir, that last one.

                                    MIKE
            No.

                                    BARTENDER
            Yes sir, house rule, for soldiers on leave.

                                    MIKE
            I thank you.

                                    BARTENDER
            Thank you, sir.

Mike puts on his cap and hurries out the door.

EXT—SIDEWALK—STREET—DAY

Mike walks quickly toward the car.

Margret emerges, turns and pulls someone forward from the rear seat. It's Jake who lurches onto the pavement, wobbling, under the influence. Behind him, pushing Jake, is Robert Berksrun, laughing.

                           MARGRET
    You two! Attenshun!

Jake and Robert come to attention. Jake yawns wearily.

                           JAKE
    God I'm tired! Been up all night, mission
    planning is doing me in!

                           ROBERT
    Come on, one more drink.

Mike moves forward.

                           MIKE (to Jake)
    Why not try sleep.

                           JAKE
    Holy cow! Look who's here!

                           MARGRET
    Mike!

                           ROBERT
    What is this?

                           MIKE (to Robert)
    What's it to you?

                           JAKE (to Robert)
    Be careful, he's got a mean right.

                           MARGRET
    Take him in, won't you Robert?

                           ROBERT (to Mike)
    I don't understand your hostility,
    (to Jake)
    Come on, old man, let's get that drink.

JAKE
See ya, Eagle Eye.

Robert and Jake climb the stairs and enter the townhouse.

MARGRET
You could have called.

MIKE
What, and miss this spectacle.

MARGRET
You damned Puritan!

MIKE
I don't like what I see here.

MARGRET
What's that supposed to mean?

MIKE
Look, I had some time, I thought we might go out for dinner, talk.

MARGRET
That's very nice, but I've got a full card for this evening, tomorrow perhaps?

MIKE
You don't care about Jake, do you?

MARGRET
That's not true.

MIKE
And you still don't believe me about the Jews, do you?

MARGRET
I don't know…I've been asking around…you may have something.

MIKE
You're damned right, you're pacifist friends are dead wrong about Germany…I've got to go.

                                    MARGRET
            Mike, come back.

Mike walks away and hails a taxi.

EXT—TRAIN STATION—DAY

Mike gets out of the taxi in front of the train station. He goes to a phone kiosk and places a call. Across the street, a hospital, nurses passing in and out.

                                    MIKE
            Mission Planning, may I speak with Colonel
            Dodge? Yes, I'll hold.

INT—MISSION PLANNING

Colonel Dodge takes the phone from an officer.

                                    DODGE
            Hello, yes, oh yes, Curtis, how are you?
            Good good, congratulations on your DFC,
            well-deserved. What's up?

EXT—TRAIN STATION—DAY

Mike draws closer to the phone, speaking more guardedly.

                                    MIKE
            Well, sir, I'm on a brief visit to London and I
            was trying to find Robert Berksrun, you
            remember? The friend of Thomas Stanford.

INT—MISSION PLANNING

Colonel Dodge picks up a private, military phone book.

                                    DODGE
            Oh yes, the statistician, he was with Mission
            Planning in London, wasn't he?

Dodge flips through the book repeatedly. He frowns.

                                    DODGE (Cont.)
            There's no listing for Berksrun. If he's not in this
            book, he's been reassigned. Sorry, Lieutenant.

EXT—PHONE KIOSK

Mike hangs up the phone. He pulls out his money roll and studies it. He spots something down the street and smiles.

EXT—CANDY SHOP—STREET—DAY

People pass by a candy store near the station.

EXT—CHILDREN'S HOSPITAL—LATER

Mike enters the hospital and carries a large box.

INT—HOSPITAL WARD—DAY

Mike helps nurses distribute candy to children in their hospital beds.

INT/EXT—TRAIN—COUNTRYSIDE—SUNSET

Mike looks out the train at the neat English farms. Suddenly, in a meadow is the wreck of an RAF Spitfire, and a white cross nearby. Then the beautiful countryside returns.

EXT—TERRACE—MANSION—EVENING

Paul, smoking a cigarette, stands on the terrace and stares off in the distance. Mike approaches him.

        MIKE
  Mind if I bum one?

        PAUL
  Holy Mary! You're back already?

        MIKE
  Should have called her first. She was busy.

        PAUL
  Yeah, well, the upper crust, they've got their
  own, ah, a-gen-da, you know. I like that word,
  heard Jake use it.

        MIKE
  He probably coined it at Yale.

Paul laughs.

                                MIKE (Cont.)
            So, what's doing?

                                PAUL
            Take a look across that meadow.

EXT—DISTANT MEADOW—EVENING

In the dusk, vague bulky shapes are moving about. Distant ENGINE sounds. A few lights flash as if from flashlights.

                                MIKE O.S.
            So, maneuvers or something?

                                PAUL O.S.
            Better. Materiel, mountains of stuff, lining the
            hedgerows, enough to sink this whole island.
            You know what that means?

                                MIKE O.S.
            The invasion.

                                PAUL O.S.
            That's right and we're here with our asses in a sling.

EXT—TERRACE—DUSK

Mike flings the cigarette down.

                                MIKE
            Not for long, pal, we're not gonna miss this.
            What's today, May what?

                                PAUL
            Thirtieth, but what will Doc say?

                                MIKE
            We'll figure something out.

Mike walks off, Paul follows. Mike stops, Paul stops.

                                MIKE
            Say, what'd you think of that Berksrun guy?
            You like him?

PAUL
I don't know…kinda your proper Englishman…wouldn't answer my question about his research…thing is, there's no reason to be secretive about statistical models. They're public knowledge for decades.

MIKE
Yeah, well…I don't like him, something gives me the creeps.

PAUL
Edith said he was a friend of Margret's from before the war, they studied in Germany together or something…Yeah, well anyway, you don't like any of the guys hanging around Margret.

Paul fakes a punch on Mike's arm and grins.

MIKE
You're are real wise guy…

INT—LIBRARY, TOWNHOUSE—LONDON—NIGHT

Jake has passed out while sitting at a long research table, his face resting on a large map of Europe. Margret and Robert stand on either side of him.

ROBERT
He's useless in this condition!

MARGRET
Don't overdo the drinking, for God's sake! Now what?

ROBERT
We keep trying…every bit of information helps. He's still our best source…I wouldn't mind him dying in the camps…

Robert gives Jake a disgusted shove. Margret looks at Robert in shock and steps between them.

MARGRET
It is true then, isn't it? The mass executions…the Jews and Gypsies?

ROBERT
Come, you aren't that naive or weak-willed, are you?

MARGRET
That's not the issue…

Robert laughs obscenely and walks out.

EXT—OXBRIDGE AFB—DAY

A taxi drops Mike and Paul with their bags at the front gate. They look at each other and shrug apprehensively as they march into Flight Headquarters.

INT—OPERATIONS OFFICE—DAY

Doc sits behind his desk and talks on the phone. Mike and Paul sit rather rigidly in chairs in front of his desk.

DOC
All of a week…It's not much of a rest!… Commander, it's your call.

Mike and Paul look at each other, dubious.

DOC (Cont.)
Yes sir, right, that's true.

Doc hangs up the phone.

DOC
All right, all right, you're back on line.

MIKE
Yes! Thanks, Doc!

DOC
Remember, you're line pilots, you don't know a damned thing about the invasion 'til you're told.

PAUL
So we're right?

DOC
Nobody tells me nothing. I've got enough problems with burnouts and more cause for low morale.

                                    MIKE
>   What happened?

                                    DOC
>   Another big loss, McCorkle—

                                    PAUL
>   McCorkle!

                                    DOC
>   Yeah, we thought he made it, he bailed out, parachuted safely to the ground.

                                    MIKE
>   So—

                                    DOC
>   So, Intelligence studied the films and the German pilot that shot McCorkle down, strafed him running down a farm road.

Mike and Paul stand up and Doc rises. They salute.

                                    MIKE
>   Thank you, sir, good to be back.

                                    DOC
>   Take easy up there, gentlemen.

EXT—SKY—FRANCE—DAY

Red Flight and other P-47s fly from France toward England.

INT/EXT—MIKE'S P-47—DAY

Mike looks around the sky over his cockpit. Suddenly he spots something.

EXT—SKY OVERHEAD

An aircraft leaves a contrail, like dashes, on and off.

                                    MIKE O.S.
>   Paul, twelve o'clock.

INT/EXT—PAUL'S P-47—DAY

Paul stares upward.

PAUL

Damn, what's that bogey?

INT/EXT—MIKE'S P-47

Mike pulls back on the stick, climbing.

MIKE

Bet you anything it's that new German jet, a pulse jet, the engine kicks on and off. Let's take it.

PAUL O.S.

I'm on your tail.

EXT—SKY—DAY

Mike, with Paul as wingman, closes on the jet.

The jet drops to a lower altitude, evading.

INT/EXT—MIKE'S P-47—DAY

Mike dives and gets a bead on the jet.

PAUL O.S.

He's losing power.

MIKE

Tough break, pal.

Mike fires several rounds that rip across the jet's fuselage. The canopy on the jet blows and the PILOT ejects.

INT/EXT—PAUL'S P-47

Paul looks out and watches the German pilot parachuting into a farm field.

PAUL

A Nazi jet pilot downed in France, say, that guy knows a helluva lot.

MIKE O.S.

You thinking about McCorkle?

PAUL

I sure am.

EXT—FIELD—DAY

The German pilot lands and jumps out of his parachute harness. He hears the ROAR of the P-47 coming over the field beyond. He starts running toward the trees.

INT/EXT—PAUL'S P-47

Paul lines him up and prepares to gun him down, his thumb on the trigger.

MIKE O.S.
Hold up! We've got help!

EXT—FIELD—FRANCE—DAY

The German pilot runs, looking back over his shoulder at the P-47s behind him. Suddenly, in front of him, a gang of angry FRENCH FARMERS with pitchforks and sticks close about him. The German pilot SCREAMS under their blows.

Mike and Paul ROAR past just overhead.

EXT—BARRACKS AREA—OXBRIDGE—EVENING

Raining. A staff car pulls up. Jake climbs out with his bag.

INT—BARRACKS ROOM—NIGHT

Mike and Paul are lying on their bunks reading. Ab's stuff is packed up in the corner, tagged for Illinois.

JAKE O.S.
Shake it up, lazy butts, we've got some flyin' to do!

PAUL
Uh oh.

Jake enters the room and throws his suitcase on his bed.

JAKE
Man, great to be a line pilot again!

Paul and Mike sit up.

JAKE (Cont.)
What kind of welcome is this?

PAUL
Welcome back, Jake, we thought maybe you had replaced Ike.

JAKE
Very funny, asshole!
(to Mike)
Hey, what happened to you, in London?

MIKE
I was on a tight schedule.

JAKE
Well, the lady's back in town, she's out at The Willows and she wants to see you.

MIKE
Sure…
JAKE (to Mike)
By the way, congratulations, ace. I knew you could do it, and a jet aircraft too! You were all the rage down at Mission Planning.

MIKE
Why are you back?

Jake smiles and wags his finger.

JAKE
Grab your jock straps, gentlemen, we're going o'er the short sea.

MIKE
When?

JAKE
Haven't a clue, but soon, it's coming, and I know which units are going where.

PAUL
Where will we be?

JAKE
Let's say this, you won't be eating blood pudding for breakfast.

                                    PAUL
        Well, I don't like snails either.

                                    MIKE
        Hey, I'll settle for good old eggs and grits.

                                    JAKE
        This is June fourth, finish your three hundred
        in June and you'll be eating breakfast in the ZI.

                                    MIKE
        That's the goal.

                                    JAKE
        Maybe in your world, Mike, but some of us are
        thinking about riding this one to Berlin. Who
        knows? I may do a second tour and earn a pair
        of gold leaves.

                                    PAUL
        Be my guest, hero!

Mike shakes his head wearily.

EXT—THE WILLOWS—NIGHT

Mike walks up to The Willows and KNOCKS at the door.

Margret opens the door. Shep comes out for a headrub.

                                    MARGRET
        I'm sorry about London.

                                    MIKE
        I am too.

                                    MARGRET
        Is there something we need to discuss?

Mike looks into her eyes, she into his.

                                    MIKE
        No.

Margret lets him in. In a moment the lights go out.

EXT—GATE—OXBRIDGE AFB—LATE AFTERNOON

Mike, Paul and Jake, dressed in flight coveralls, cross the road from the hangar side to the barracks side. They carry their post-mission eggs.

          PAUL
Boy, that's was a routine mission, creepy how quiet things are.

          JAKE
Just sit tight, gentlemen, our moment of glory is comin'…say, I've got dinner at The Willows this evening with Robert and Margret…
(to Mike)
you don't mind, old chum, unfinished London business.

          MIKE
A magnum of champagne, no doubt.

          JAKE
Touche, mon ami! Let's not forget, all for one, and one for all…anything pops, let me know—

Paul stumbles, drops an egg, splattering on road. Jake laughs, Mike smiles sympathetically.

          PAUL (to Mike)
Jesus! Come on, let's clean up and go to the Officer's Mess.

INT—BEDROOM—THE WILLOWS—LATE AFTERNOON

Margret storms into the bedroom followed by Robert Berksrun. She throws open the radio closet and tears at the wires.

          MARGRET
I've had it, you hear! Enough!

          ROBERT
Stop it, stop it!

Shep begins barking at Robert. Robert kicks him out of the room and slams the door. He snatches Margret around to face him, she tries to break free. He slaps her across her eyes and she recoils in shock, in pain. He shakes her.

                              ROBERT
I'm warning you, Margret! We're not playing
games here! We're well past any point of return...

                              MARGRET
Everyone's dying, Robert!

                              ROBERT
Yes, yes, there must be sacrifice in war, and we
have no choice now.

Robert shoves her in chair before the radio. Margret sobs.

                              ROBERT (Cont.)
Get yourself together, Margret, Jake will be
here soon...

                              MARGRET
I can't face him...tell him anything...please,
take him to town or something...

                              ROBERT
Very well...

Robert glances into his attache case, open on the desk, inside a pistol.

INT—BARRACKS HALLWAY—EVENING

OFFICERS are wandering the hall, talking, joking, when the door opens and in comes a MILITARY POLICE CAPTAIN.

                              CAPTAIN
Gentlemen, the base is now being sealed,
Commander's orders. All passes are canceled,
all personnel are confined to base.

Captain steps aside as other MP's enter with rifles and begin handing them out to pilots. Mike and Paul step into the hallway and receive their weapons.

INT—MIKE & PAUL'S ROOM

They reenter room.

                              PAUL
This is it, the invasion...is there a phone at
The Willows?

              MIKE
No, the main house but not The Willows.

              PAUL
Jake needs to be notified.

              MIKE
I'll go.

              PAUL
Are you sure?

              MIKE
Yeah…

EXT—THE WILLOWS—EARLY EVENING

Mike walks up to the house, its lights on, and he knocks on the door. Shep BARKS, the door opens, Margret holding it open. Mike pets Shep.

              MARGRET
Mike…

              MIKE
I'm looking for Jake.

              MARGRET
He went to King John's with Robert for a drink. I just wasn't up to it.

She turns her face slightly, a black eye.

              MIKE
What happened?

              MARGRET
Oh, I did this hunting with Robert, slipped and fell on a stile.

              MIKE
You're lucky you weren't shot.

              MARGRET
Yes, or Robert, it was quite troubling…

                                              MIKE
        Well, I've got to go, the time...
                                              MARGRET
        Please come in, just for a moment.

Mike looks back toward the base, hesitates.

                                              MIKE
        A minute, that's all.

INT—LIVING ROOM

Mike enters and stands, waiting.

                                              MARGRET
        Won't you sit down.

                                              MIKE
        I can't.

                                              MARGRET
        I see...I'm sorry things haven't worked out. I
        do believe you now...about what's happening
        to the Jews and Gypsies...it is true...I'm so
        sorry I didn't believe you...We were so far
        apart on so many things, and yet—

Margret steps closer to him.

                                              MIKE
        And yet we could be lovers?

Margret touches his face tenderly.

                                              MARGRET
        Yes.

Mike kisses her and then releases her. She's crying.

                                              MIKE
        What's wrong?

                                              MARGRET
        I'm afraid I won't see you again.

> MIKE
> Why?

> MARGRET
> Because, it's so dangerous, the odds are against you.

Mike looks over her shoulder toward the dining room table.

INT—DINING ROOM—THE WILLOWS

On the table, maps of the French coast, marked up in red.

INT—LIVING ROOM—THE WILLOWS

Mike's expression goes blank. He lets go of her.

> MIKE
> The odds are changing, all the time. I'll be back, Margret.

Mike opens the door and backs out.

> MARGRET
> Tomorrow, Robert and I return to London midday.

> MIKE
> Can't you stay over a few days?

> MARGRET
> I don't think so, no, not now. I have to finish things in London.

> MIKE
> I'll find you when this is over.

> MARGRET
> Au revoir.

> MIKE O.S.
> Au revoir.

EXT—ROAD TO BASE—NIGHT

Mike walks along the road. Suddenly a car appears at high speed, Mike has to jump aside, gravel sprays against him.

EXT/INT—CAR WINDSHIELD—NIGHT

Robert Berksrun is behind the wheel, his face taut, concentrated. He glances at Mike and flashes by.

EXT—ROAD—NIGHT

Mike watches Robert race away, then jogs toward the base.

INT—BARRACKS ROOM—NIGHT

Mike bursts into the bedroom. Jake is undressing, drunkenly pulling his shirt off. Paul sits on his own bed listening to a RADIO ADDRESS by Winston Churchill.

>   MIKE (to Jake)
> What did you tell Berksrun?
>
>   JAKE
> Whaaat?
>
>   MIKE
> What did you tell Berksrun about the invasion?
>
>   JAKE
> Nothing he didn't already know. It's pretty obvious where the action will be, if you know European geography. Anyway, Robert's privy to invasion plans.
>
>   MIKE
> Really? A statistician with Mission Planning who's not with Mission Planning anymore?
>
>   JAKE
> What are you saying?
>
>   MIKE
> You drink too much, you spill your guts to impress people.
>
>   JAKE
> You calling me a security risk?
>
>   MIKE
> Yeah, yeah, you could be. What did you tell them? What was on the maps at The Willows?

Mike grabs him and pins him against the wall. Jake struggles, but can't free himself.

                    JAKE
    Buzz off!

In support, Paul appears beside Mike.

                    PAUL
    Tell us, Jake.

Jake slumps slightly.

                    JAKE
    I don't know, best guesses where the invasion forces would be, ninth air force over right away, then the eighth much later—

                    MIKE
    You told them where?

                    JAKE
    Yeah, those big farm fields on the Cherbourg Peninsula.

                    PAUL
    Jesus.

                    JAKE
    Margret and Robert are loyal Brits!

                    MIKE
    I don't give a damn, you shouldn't tell a soul.

Jake breaks free.

                    MIKE (Cont.)
    That farm area was clear of German forces yesterday.

                    JAKE
    So? They're all over the place.

                    MIKE
    We better not run into big trouble there tomorrow.

                    JAKE
    Yeah, right! There's no connection, you can't prove a thing.

                                PAUL
        Why do we have to prove anything?

                                JAKE
        Report me, then! Go ahead, try to ruin me!
        Take your best shot!

Jake, drunkenly, throws himself in his bunk. Paul and Mike look at each other and shake their heads in disbelief.

INT—BEDROOM—THE WILLOWS—MIDNIGHT

The secret compartment is open and Margret and Robert are hunched over the radio again, Robert with the maps of the French Coast, Margret tapping out code, haltingly, using a code book.

She's crying, tries to get up, Berksrun snatches her back into her chair. She gasps and taps out the code.

EXT—OXBRIDGE AFB—4 A.M.

INSERT TITLE: JUNE 6, 1944

Pilots are gathered in the mission briefing room. Mike, Paul, and Jake sit near each other. Jake looks hungover.

The Commander, with a group of INTELLIGENCE OFFICERS around him with charts and stats, points with a stick at the coast of France on the map.

                                COMMANDER
        We fly all day as long as there's light. Each
        squadron has its assignments for invasion support.

                                JAKE
        Sir?

                                COMMANDER
        Yes, Captain Russell?

                                JAKE
        What's the enemy activity status in the
        Cherbourg peninsula area?

Commander glances at Intelligence Officers. They shrug as if nothing unusual is happening. Commander uses pointer to indicate the geography.

                              COMMANDER
            Intelligence reports Nazi troop movement will
            be away from the Cherbourg peninsula, moving
            rapidly out of there to counterattack at the inva-
            sion beaches down here. That's why we chose
            this area for the ninth, last place they'll be…in
            any numbers, anyway. They'll be moving out,
            we'll be moving in…right after our paratroopers
            drop in later this week…Any more questions?

The room is very still, quiet.

                              COMMANDER (Cont.)
            Gentlemen, this is a great day, a great moment
            in history. I wish you the best of luck, you can
            only bring honor on us. God bless you.

                              JUNIOR OFFICER
            Attenshunt!

All stand and salute, the Commander salutes smartly and exits quickly.

EXT—RUNWAY—DAWN

Raining. Flights of P-47s take off.

EXT—SKY—CHANNEL—DAWN

The P-47s stream toward the coast of France. The rain stops over the channel.

INT/EXT—MIKE'S P-47—FRENCH COAST—DAWN

Mike looks out and down.

EXT—FRENCH COAST—DAWN

Invasion forces land on the beaches. Fighting is fierce.

INT/EXT—PAUL'S P-47—DAWN

Paul glances out and checks coordinates.

                              PAUL
            There's our target.

EXT/INT—MIKE'S P-47—DAWN

Mike's plane dives with others in flight.

EXT—BUNKERS/DEPOTS—DAWN

The P-47s dive bomb, their bombs blowing up German forces' materiel depots; ammo bunkers explode violently. German soldiers run for cover.

EXT—RUNWAY—FRENCH COAST—MORNING

German fighters taxi and take-off.

INT/EXT—MIKE'S P-47—MORNING

Mike lines up a row of taxiing planes and fires away. German planes are hit, one explodes in flames. Mike pulls up to avoid exploding debris.

INT/EXT—PAUL'S P-47—MORNING

Paul dives, shooting up another section of the aerodrome. Flak explodes around him, jarring his plane.

INT/EXT—JAKE'S P-47—MORNING

Jake looks exhausted, nervous, he's sweating; he dives and shoots up a row of parked planes. His plane is hit by the PING-PING of small ground fire. He pulls up and away.

INT/EXT—MIKE'S P-47—LATER

Mike dives at a congested convoy of German trucks moving toward the beachhead. He fires, trucks exploding, troops running into the fields and ditches.

INT/EXT—PAUL'S P-47

Paul dives and shoots up the truck convoy.

INT/EXT—JAKE'S P-47

Jake fires away at the convoy and pulls up.

                                           JAKE
          Okay you guys, time to check the peninsula
          and clear my name.

INT/EXT—MIKE'S P-47—MORNING

Mike looks out cockpit at Paul nearby. Paul shrugs.

                                           MIKE
          Let's do it, let's settle this.

INT/EXT—JAKE'S P-47—MORNING

Jake pulls ahead of them and streaks toward the coast and the peninsula. German truck convoys exit the peninsula, inland, in the distance.

                JAKE
  There they go, just like intelligence predicted, they're abandoning the peninsula.

EXT—COASTAL PENINSULA—FRANCE—MORNING

The threesome approaches the end of the peninsula, which is flat with wide meadows running near the shore. Copses of trees line the boundaries of the huge farming fields. Small figures can be seen working in the plowed fields.

                JAKE O.S.
  This will be perfect for the Ninth's advance airfields.

INT/EXT—MIKE'S P-47—MORNING

Mike swings down lower.

                MIKE
  There's some smoke, a train on the spur line.

EXT—PENINSULA—FRANCE—DAY

Along the spur line is a train, and the train has Red Cross markings, hospital cars.

INT/EXT—JAKE'S P-47—MORNING

Jake rolls over, observing the train.

                JAKE
  A Red Cross train, hospital train.

                MIKE O.S.
  What the hell's it doing out here?

                JAKE
  Oh come off it!

Jake is sweating, his hand shakes, he wipes his hand on the parachute talisman. Jake dives toward the train.

INT/EXT—MIKE'S P-47—MORNING

Mike follows Jake, and dives down, skimming over the train.

EXT—TRAIN—SIDING—MORNING

The train appears to be idling, Red Cross markings all over it. An armed soldier ducks into the caboose.

INT/EXT—JAKE'S P-47

Jake looks back at Mike and Paul trailing him.

>   JAKE
> You see, big shot!

INT/EXT—MIKE'S P-47

Mike looks down at the train, and circles, coming lower over the fields. He looks down at the "farmers" in the fields near the train.

EXT—FIELDS

The so-called "farmers" are digging holes, stacks of disc-like objects and wiring in the field rows. A couple of farmers start running toward the train.

INT/EXT—MIKE'S P-47

Mike pulls up.

>   MIKE
> Sonofabitch! They're planting mines! Let's take'em!

INT/EXT—JAKE'S P-47

Jake looks confused, disoriented.

>   JAKE
> Noooo, it can't be!

He swings wide, observing the fields below.

INT/EXT—PAUL'S P-47

Paul follows Mike.

>   MIKE O.S.
> Paul, take the last caboose, I'll hit the engine.

INT/EXT—MIKE'S P-47

Mike dives and fires at the boiler on the locomotive. It erupts in a giant plume of steam.

INT/EXT—PAUL'S P-47

Paul dives at the rear of the train.

EXT—REAR OF TRAIN

The sides fall down revealing flak guns mounted inside. They start firing.

INT/EXT—PAUL'S P-47

Paul rakes the train, explosions rock the cars, and troops scatter across the fields.

INT/EXT—MIKE'S P-47

Mike glances over at Paul. Mike's face shows shock.

EXT—TRAIN SIDING

The train sits parallel to a string of high tension wires.

INT/EXT—PAUL'S P-47

Paul is so intent on firing into the train, he doesn't see the approaching towers' lines.

MIKE O.S.
Pull up! Pull up!

Paul's face is in shock as the wires come at him. He jerks the stick over.

EXT—HIGH TENSION TOWERS

Paul's P-47, wings vertical to the ground, slices through the wires, setting off sparks, electrical explosions.

INT/EXT—PAUL'S P-47

Paul fights for control, his wings slashed. The plane loses power and he belly lands in a nearby field.

When he comes to a stop, the engine bursts into flame. Paul slides back the canopy and climbs out.

EXT—FIELD

Across the field, German soldiers with guns are running toward him, stopping and FIRING.

Paul runs toward a nearby dirt farm road.

INT/EXT—MIKE'S P-47

Mike sees the soldiers and Paul's flight.

        MIKE
  Jake! Goddammit, respond!

INT/EXT—JAKE'S P-47

Jake only has eyes on the train, the flak gun cars, the burning cars. He's mumbling.

        JAKE
  You're going to report this?

        MIKE O.S.
  No, you are! Cover me!

Jake looks out at Paul running, he shakes his head no, and turns back toward the train.

        JAKE
  Paul's a dead man!

        MIKE O.S.
  Jake! Jake! Cover me!

INT/EXT—MIKE'S P-47

Mike rakes the field behind Paul. The troops go down.

Mike pulls up and swings low over the road, lines it up and cuts his power...

EXT—FIELD/ROAD

Eagle Eye lands on the road. Mike throws back the cockpit, and throws out his parachute (not room for Paul and chute).

Paul leaps over a fence, troops firing after him, and jumps up on the wing. Mike taxis as Paul climbs in the cockpit.

INT/EXT—MIKE'S P-47

Paul sits down and Mike has to squat on Paul's lap to fit in. Bullets PING off the plane.

        PAUL
  Crazy sonofabitch! God love you!

They duck as Mike accelerates for take-off. More shells strike the plane.

EXT—ROAD

Mike takes off slowly. Several troops block the road and fire directly point-blank, then dive for cover at the last minute as the plane, wings swaying wildly, pulls up, and just clears the trees.

INT/EXT—MIKE'S P-47

Mike gets on the radio.

>   MIKE (to Jake)
> Let's clear out, cover me back over the Channel.

>   PAUL
> He's going after that flak gun.

>   MIKE
> Jake!

INT/EXT—JAKE'S P-47

Jake, at a low altitude, flies right at the flak car, firing into it, the flak coming in streams at him.

>   JAKE
> Traitors!

An explosion in the cockpit throws him back in his seat, the parachute talisman flames up; blood covers his chest, but with his last bit of mental focus he flies the fighter straight at the rear of the train.

EXT—FLAK CAR—TRAIN

Jake's P-47 slams into the train, an enormous explosion destroys the rear of the train, setting off a chain reaction of explosions down the track and out in the fields where the land mines explode.

INT/EXT—MIKE'S P-47

Mike and Paul look on Jake's death. Mike's plane sputters, having engine trouble, the plane flying a few hundred feet off the Channel.

>   PAUL
> He died taking out a target of opportunity.

>   MIKE
> Yeah, and I got another target near Oxbridge.

Paul looks confused but shrugs it off.

INT/EXT—MIKE'S P-47—SKY/CHANNEL—DAY

Mike takes up a heading toward England. Paul changes radio channels, but STATIC jams the airwaves. They're flying lower and lower, losing altitude.

> PAUL
> They're jamming us!

> MIKE
> Dammit!

There's a dull, metallic thud. Paul looks behind.

> PAUL
> We got company! The wrong kind!

EXT—SKY—CHANNEL—DAY

A German ME-109 is behind them and firing.

INT/EXT—MIKE'S P-47—DAY

Mike and Paul crouch down as the plane is peppered with strikes from the German.

> PAUL
> Holy Jesus!

Smoke and a small fire erupt in the cockpit. Mike with gloved hand beats out the electrical fire.

EXT/INT—MIKE'S P-47—DAY

The plane is hit again and again with shells. Part of the canopy explodes, then parts of the engine cowl, fragments of metal flying off. Smoke erupts from the engine slightly. Mike and Paul keep low. Mike struggles with the controls.

INT/EXT—GERMAN'S ME-109—DAY

The German PILOT gets the "Eagle Eye" insignia in his cross hairs and fires. Insignia takes hits before Mike can evade the German, swinging plane sluggishly from side to side.

INT/EXT—MIKE'S P-47—DAY

Mike's face is cut slightly from flying fragments.

                              MIKE
      Come on, baby! Come on!

                              PAUL
      He won't stay with us to the coast!

Another burst rips through the plane, more metal flying off.

INT/EXT—GERMAN'S ME-109

The German pilot fires another round striking at the wingroot. He frowns as he misses direct hits, Mike twisting sluggishly from side to side.

The pilot, angry now, lines up for another shot directly into the cockpit. He fires and the cockpit glass, much of it, explodes, but then his guns stop firing.

The German presses the firing button repeatedly, frustrated, he's out of ammo.

INT/EXT—MIKE'S P-47—DAY

The wind rushes in as Mike cuts back the engine. The German fighter plane pulls alongside. Mike and Paul look his way.

                              MIKE
      Fly high and keep your nose in the wind!

EXT—GERMAN FIGHTER

The German pilot shakes his head in frustration, grins, salutes and peels away for France.

INT/EXT—MIKE'S P-47—DAY

Below them the English coast approaches and the emergency landing base. Paul kisses the cross around his neck.

                              PAUL
      Thank you, God, thank you!

                              MIKE
      Thank God *and* Pratt and Whitney. That
      engine's a miracle!

                              PAUL
      Amen!

Paul looks at the penciled total of hours, 250, on Mike's instrument panel, taps it with his finger.

                              PAUL (Cont.)
          You're in luck, I heard they're rolling back the
          combat hours after D-day. You may go home
          when I do.

Underneath, the emergency base passes by. Paul cranes his neck watching it fade.

                              PAUL (Cont.)
         Hey, there's the landing strip? What're you doin'?

                              MIKE
         We're pushing on to Oxbridge.

                              PAUL
         Are you crazy? We'll never make it!

                              MIKE
         We'll make it, we gotta.

EXT—RUNWAY—OXBRIDGE—MORNING

Fire trucks race to the runway. Mike's plane, engine smoking, heads for the runway, both wing wheels locked up.

                              MIKE O.S.
         The hydraulics are gone.

                              PAUL O.S.
         Holy Mary!

INT/EXT—MIKE'S P-47—MORNING

Paul crouches down and clutches his cross. His hand is covered with blood, and he sees his side is bleeding.

Mike brings the plane down, the wings wavering, and then carefully bellies in along the runway. Sparks fly and he slides it off the runway into the grass.

EXT—RUNWAY END—OXBRIDGE—NOON

Mike climbs out quickly, pulling Paul. Smoke issues from the fuselage now, as they stumble away. The plane goes up in flames, the fire trucks pouring on water.

EXT—MEDIC AREA—HANGAR

Paul's side is covered in blood. Mike sees Paul to the medics. A young MEDIC rips open Mario's flight suit.

> MEDIC
> Hell! No arteries hit! You'll live!

Paul smiles weakly and lays back on the stretcher. The medic stares at Mike's facial wound which is superficial, and hands him a piece of gauze. Mike pushes it aside and spots a jeep.

Mike commandeers it from an enlisted man and drives off.

EXT—GATE AREA—OPERATIONS

Lauren sees Mike race off the base in the jeep and she runs into Operations Headquarters.

EXT—ROAD TO THE WILLOWS—DAY

Mike races in the jeep along the road.

INT—BEDROOM—THE WILLOWS—DAY

Margret smashes the radio, pulling it from its compartment. Robert Berksrun watches her and laughs.

> ROBERT
> Go ahead! We're finished now! That's it!

> MARGRET
> You bastard! Get out!

> ROBERT
> Oh no…you're going back to London with me. You're in no condition to stay here by yourself. I want you with our friends in London…'til you come to your senses!

> MARGRET
> Go to hell, I'm finished! I'm turning myself in!

Shep growls from the other room and starts toward Robert. He pulls a pistol from his pocket and fires into the other room. Shep YELPS, his whimpering fading…

Margret glances at her gun rack and jumps for her guns.

EXT—YARD—THE WILLOWS—DAY

Mike pulls into the yard. GUNSHOT. There's another car in the yard, front door open, luggage piled haphazardly.

EXT/INT—DOORWAY

Mike pauses briefly in the doorway, hears a WHIMPERING, and sees Shep lying on the floor nearby, blood on his head.

Mike looks around and spots Robert Berksrun in the dining room. Robert crams maps and papers into a briefcase.

>   MIKE
> What's going on?

Robert jumps in surprise. He keeps his hands inside the open attache case.

>   ROBERT
> There's been a hunting accident—

>   MIKE
> Where's Margret!?

Robert pauses, his face pale, he swallows hard. Mike rushes into the bedroom.

INT—BEDROOM

Margret lies on the floor in a pool of blood. He rushes to her side. She has a bad wound in the chest. Her eyes blink, her eyes roll as Mike lifts her head up.

>   MIKE
> Oh no! Oh no!

>   MARGRET
> I'm sorry, Mike.

>   MIKE (to Robert)
> Get some help!
> (to Margret)
> Sorry?

>   MARGRET
> I…I…made a great mistake, Mike, forgive me…

                                    MIKE
            Shush.

Mike spots the radio equipment in the open closet, smashed. Mike puts her down gently and rushes to the bedroom door.

INT—DININGROOM—DAY

Robert holds a pistol on Mike.

                                    ROBERT
            Don't move, Mike!

Mike freezes.

                                    MIKE
            Get some help, for God's sake!

                                    ROBERT
            No, it's too late for Margret.

                                    MIKE
            Are you insane?

                                    ROBERT
            You're in, or you're out, Mike. Margret should
            have known that, you can't have it both ways.

                                    MIKE
            You sorry sonofabitch! You'll never get away...

                                    ROBERT
            I've got friends in London...powerful friends
            who will see me through this...Sorry, old chum,
            we can't leave clues—

Shep growls, Mike jumps to the side of the door, Robert fires, the slug grazes his left arm. Mike slams and bolts the bedroom door. Slugs BURST through the door. A silence follows, then a CAR ENGINE ROARS to life.

Mike goes to Margret. She shudders and smiles up at him.

                                    MIKE
            He's gone, you'll be okay.

                              MARGRET
    D-Day, is it working?

                              MIKE
    Yes, shhh.

                              MARGRET
    Was Jake a hero?

                              MIKE
    Yes, he was a hero.

Outside, the CAR ROARS away from The Willows. Mike looks over and spots Margret's hunting rifles. He goes to the gun rack. In great pain from the arm wound, he picks up a rifle, tears open a shell box and jams a shell in the rifle.

He steps up to the large bay windows and kicks them open.

INT—ROAD VIEW

The open windows expose the little pond, the meadow and road beyond. Mike takes aim and tracks Berksrun in his car.

EXT/INT—GUN SCOPE VIEW

Mike stares along the sights and lines up Berksrun…Mike squints, his vision blurring.

                              MARGRET O.S.
        Mike…

INT—MIKE IN WINDOW

Mike glances back at her and then grimly refocuses on sighting the car. He grits his teeth focusing his vision.

EXT/INT—WINDSHIELD—CAR

Berksrun drives furiously, his face grim, obsessive.

EXT—CAR—ROAD

The car races along the road. A SHOT RINGS OUT, GLASS SHATTERS, the car speeds along on course, but then it veers off the road as if airborne for a second, then slams into a ditch, the HORN SOUNDING without interruption.

EXT/INT—WINDSHIELD—CAR

The windshield is smashed, Berksrun slumped over the wheel, a ghastly, mortal head wound.

INT/EXT—BEDROOM—THE WILLOWS

Mike observes the wreck, drops the rifle and rushes to Margret. He sits beside Margret and touches her cheek.

> MARGRET
> This fall, you and I, deer hunting…
> (looks past Mike)
> and Uncle and my brother…oh, here they are now!

Mike looks and sees nothing but a bullet-riddled door. Margret GURGLES and slumps.

> MIKE
> Easy now.

> MARGRET
> Hold me, please, hold me…

Mike puts his arms around her, hugs her, kisses her neck, she kisses him once on the neck, smiles and slumps, dead. Mike trembles, holding her lifeless body.

EXT—PARADE GROUNDS—OXBRIDGE AFB—DAY

KING & QUEEN OF ENGLAND review the squadrons of pilots accompanied by a cluster of GENERALS. The public looks on, Edith and Lauren watch proudly.

EXT—MIKE'S SQUADRON

Mike and Paul stand at attention as the King presents Paul with a medal.

> KING
> We thank you so much for your bravery, for helping us.

> PAUL
> Thank you, sir, an honor to serve.

The King and Queen and Generals shake hands with Paul.

The group passes to Mike, his left arm in a sling. A General whispers into the King's ear, who whispers to the Queen, who looks at Mike sympathetically.

The King presents Mike with his medal and whispers.

> **KING**
> I'm so sorry, young man, a terrible loss, if there's anything I can do.

> **MIKE**
> Yes sir, thank you, sir...well, there is one small matter.

Mike whispers in the royal ear.

INT—INTERROGATION OFFICE—DAY

American and British Intelligence OFFICERS, including (now) Major Watson, sit around a conference table with Mike, who stiffly, somewhat impatiently smokes a cigarette. Lauren, wearing a British officer's uniform, sits with them and looks at Mike sympathetically.

> **BRITISH OFFICER #1**
> You see, Lieutenant, Military Intelligence must track civilian security problems as well, especially as we English have a rather murky past with the Germans. We've intermarried, even borrowed their royalty in fact, and there are inevitably sympathizers on both sides, people caught in the middle.

> **BRITISH OFFICER #2**
> And some of these collaborators are quite dangerous and unpredictable, like Robert Berksrun... I'm afraid Miss Toland was duped into being a local gathering post for a rather sinister network, and now we've broken that circuit, thanks to your unexpected effort...

Mike crushes out his cigarette and shifts uncomfortably.

> **BRITISH OFFICER #3**
> Well, sorry to keep you, Lieutenant. I imagine you are rather eager to pack things in, good luck.

Mike and the Intelligence Officers stand, salute, and Mike, a brief glance at Lauren, exits. The Intelligence Officers soberly watch him go.

INT—OFFICER'S CLUB—NIGHT

The pilots perform the candle ceremony in memory of Jake. Mike, with Paul's assistance, blacks in "Capt. J. Russell" on the roofbeam, the date is D-Day, "6-6-44." They salute and stand in silence.

EXT—DOCK—QUEEN MARY—EVENING

A foggy evening on the dock, American military are boarding the Queen Mary, papers in hand. Mike and Paul stand with Lauren and Edith. Paul kisses and hugs Edith passionately, clearly suffering the separation.

> EDITH
> Paul, I'm not going to think about the time. The war will end soon.

> PAUL
> If it's not, I'll come back for another tour.

> EDITH
> You will do nothing of the kind! You stay in Boston and wait for me.

Lauren and Mike step away to give them a moment.

> MIKE
> So, she's visiting after the war?

> LAUREN
> Yes, and it may be more than a visit. We've been talking it over, and I may accompany her. I've never seen America, except in the movies.

> MIKE
> Then you three should drive down to Virginia for a visit.

> LAUREN
> I'd like that very much…I—

Lauren looks at Mike with genuine affection and sympathy.

LAUREN (Cont.)
I'm so sorry about everything, not being able
to tell you the truth, Margret and everything.
Edith knew nothing of course…I wish—

MIKE
Don't wish, it's too late, it all happened so fast.
I don't blame anyone…I'm just praying for the
killing to end…

LAUREN
It's a madness…

Mike nods in agreement. A whistle BLOWS, last call. Paul and Edith break in. Edith kisses Mike and hugs him.

EDITH (to Mike)
I'll miss you. Keep Paul away from the women
on board.

PAUL
Oh, listen to this!

MIKE
No shipboard romances, yes mam.

Paul kisses Lauren and Edith a final time and starts up the gangplank. Edith cries and looks away.

MIKE (to Lauren)
Well…goodbye…come to see me after the war,
won't you? Give you a free ride in my biplane…

LAUREN
You promise?

MIKE
Promise.

LAUREN
It's a date then, Eagle Eye.

Mike kisses Lauren with a bit more passion than a formal farewell kiss. He turns and ascends the gangplank.

EXT—QUEEN MARY—EVENING

Foggy. Mike and Paul stand on the railing and wave to Edith and Lauren, standing among the crowd of well-wishers.

                        MIKE V.O.
       I wasn't sure I wanted to face life in the ZI, my
       old Zone of the Interior, my country tis of
       thee, but I was finished with my stretch in the
       E.T.O., except for the memories and—

INT—BAGGAGE AREA—QUEEN MARY

Workmen push a wooden crate into position in the hold; in metal lockers, the labeled boxed possessions of deceased pilots. Shep looks out apprehensively from the crate at his new surroundings. The King of England's transit seal is marked on his crate: "By Order of His Majesty," and the address to Culpeper, Virginia.

                        MIKE V.O.
       —a certain soft spot, an old friend from The
       Willows.

EXT—QUEEN MARY

The ship fog horn SOUNDS. Mike and Paul remain on the rail with other troops as tugboats push the Queen Mary away into the harbor fog.

THE END

FADE OUT:

P.O. Box 776
Needham, MA 02494
phone: 781-559-8245
http://www.jimstallings.com
email: jim@jimstallings.com

0-595-29841-9

Printed in Great Britain
by Amazon